The Illustrated World of
OCEANS

The Illustrated World of
OCEANS

SUSAN WELLS

SILVER BURDETT GINN

OCEANS

ISBN 0-382-33707-7   95 96 97 98 99 00 -MZ- 6 5 4 3 2 1

British Library Cataloguing in Publication Data for this book are available from the British Library

CONTENTS

World Oceans   6

The Circulating Waters   8
Ocean Weather   10
The violent hurricane   10
Tidal ranges   12
Ice at sea   12
Ocean Legends   14

The Ocean Floor   16
Continental movements   18

The Living Oceans   22
Earliest Life   24
The first fish on land   24
Burgess shale fossils   25
Levels of Ocean Life   26
Plankton and the food web   27
Invertebrates   28
The beautiful pirates   29
Fish   30
Great white shark   30
Angel fish   31
Mammals   32
A poorly adapted mammal   32
Ending the hunt   34
Birds   36
A guillemot bazaar   36

Ocean Migrations   38

The Ocean Margins   40
Life on the rocks   43
Coral Reefs   44

Exploring the Oceans   46
The Spirit of St. Louis   48
The voyages of Captain Cook   49
Floating castles   50
Shipwrecks   51

Exploiting the Oceans   52
Krill   52
Taking the catch   54
Polluting the oceans   56
Rainbow Warrior   59

Glossary   60

Index   62

WORLD OCEANS

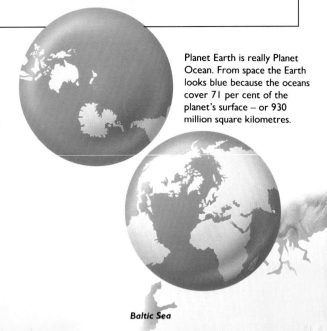

THE EARTH has more ocean than any other planet in our solar system. The oceans are largely responsible for our climate, they are where life began, and they provide us with food and numerous other essential products.

Planet Earth is really Planet Ocean. From space the Earth looks blue because the oceans cover 71 per cent of the planet's surface – or 930 million square kilometres.

The total volume of the oceans is about 1,400 million cubic kilometres but this is not evenly spread over the planet. Most is in the southern hemisphere. There are five major oceans. The Pacific is the largest, covering 32 per cent of the globe, with an area of 430 million square kilometres, more than all the land put together. It is also the deepest ocean, with an average depth of 4,200 metres, but plunging over 11 kilometres in the Mindanao Trench. The Atlantic is only half as big, with an area of 80 million square kilometres. It is also shallower, with a maximum depth of

Baltic Sea

ASIA

Persian Gulf

Red Sea

Arabian Sea

Bay of Bengal

Rain forests of the sea
Coral reefs grow in the warm, coastal waters of the tropics. They can be thought of as the rain forests of the sea because of the enormous variety of plants and animals found on them *(see pages 44-45).*

NINETY EAST RIDGE ——

INDIAN OCEAN

9,558 metres in the Puerto Rico Trench. The Indian Ocean lies in the southern hemisphere and covers 73.5 million square kilometres. The small Arctic Ocean is almost entirely surrounded by land, and is usually covered by ice, 3–4 metres thick. The Antarctic, or Southern, Ocean is larger and surrounds the continent of Antarctica. Two-thirds of it freezes in winter. Seas are smaller, shallower areas of ocean, partly surrounded by land, and include the Mediterranean, Baltic, Bering, and Caribbean.

Sperm whales
Sperm whales live in all oceans. They are the most numerous of the great whales but have been massively hunted for their oil *(see pages 34-35).* The head of the sperm whale is about one-third of the animal's length. Sperm whales have the largest brains of all mammals.

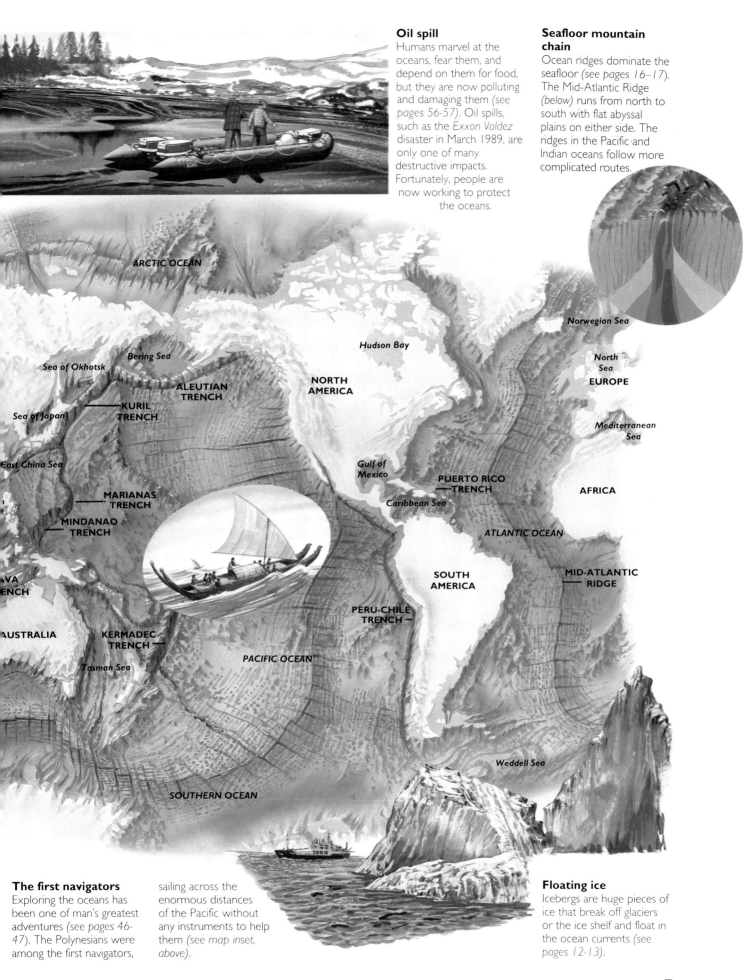

Oil spill
Humans marvel at the oceans, fear them, and depend on them for food, but they are now polluting and damaging them *(see pages 56-57)*. Oil spills, such as the *Exxon Valdez* disaster in March 1989, are only one of many destructive impacts. Fortunately, people are now working to protect the oceans.

Seafloor mountain chain
Ocean ridges dominate the seafloor *(see pages 16–17)*. The Mid-Atlantic Ridge *(below)* runs from north to south with flat abyssal plains on either side. The ridges in the Pacific and Indian oceans follow more complicated routes.

ARCTIC OCEAN

Hudson Bay

Bering Sea

Sea of Okhotsk

ALEUTIAN TRENCH

NORTH AMERICA

Norwegian Sea

North Sea

EUROPE

Sea of Japan

KURIL TRENCH

East China Sea

Mediterranean Sea

MARIANAS TRENCH

Gulf of Mexico

PUERTO RICO TRENCH

AFRICA

MINDANAO TRENCH

Caribbean Sea

ATLANTIC OCEAN

VA ENCH

SOUTH AMERICA

MID-ATLANTIC RIDGE

PERU-CHILE TRENCH

AUSTRALIA

KERMADEC TRENCH

Tasman Sea

PACIFIC OCEAN

Weddell Sea

SOUTHERN OCEAN

The first navigators
Exploring the oceans has been one of man's greatest adventures *(see pages 46-47)*. The Polynesians were among the first navigators, sailing across the enormous distances of the Pacific without any instruments to help them *(see map inset, above)*.

Floating ice
Icebergs are huge pieces of ice that break off glaciers or the ice shelf and float in the ocean currents *(see pages 12-13)*.

7

THE CIRCULATING WATERS

THE atmosphere and the oceans form a single system that creates weather, climate, currents, and waves. Ocean waters store heat from the sun during the day and in summer, and release it at night and in winter. This causes daily variations of land and sea breezes as well as seasonal monsoon cycles.

Currents transport heat around the oceans, together with oxygen, nutrients, plants, animals, turtles, young and migrating animals. The surface currents in the top 45 metres are produced by winds. The Earth's rotation deflects the water movement so that it flows at an angle to the wind direction. In the northern hemisphere, it flows to the right of the wind, creating clockwise currents, and in the south to the left, creating anticlockwise currents.

The North and South Equatorial currents flow from east to west across the oceans. In the Atlantic, the northern current flows into the Gulf of Mexico and then north and

Upwellings
Upwellings form where currents part (divergence), or where winds blow surface waters away from the coast. In both cases, cold, nutrient-rich water is able to rise. This occurs mostly on the west coasts of continents, or in the Southern Ocean. Upwellings provide food for many plants and animals, so they are often important fishing grounds.

The cold Peru (or Humboldt) current flows north along the western coast of South America, creating an upwelling off the coast of Peru where fish are very abundant.

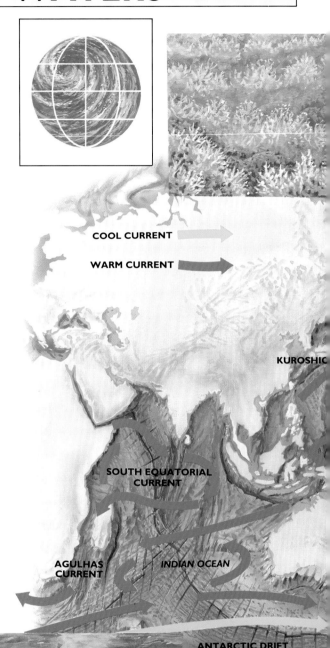

COOL CURRENT

WARM CURRENT

KUROSHIO

SOUTH EQUATORIAL CURRENT

AGULHAS CURRENT

INDIAN OCEAN

ANTARCTIC DRIFT

The visit of 'El Niño'

Periodically, a mass of warm water flows south along the west coast of South America, swamping the upwelling. This often happens just after Christmas, so it is called 'El Niño', or 'The Child'. It brings with it torrential rain, and the food chain is drastically altered. In the 1982–83 El Niño, corals were bleached white (below, left) and tens of thousands of animals in the Galapagos died. There were also droughts as far afield as Australia and northeast Brazil.

east as the Gulf Stream. It flows at up to 225 kilometres a day, with numerous complex eddies and gyres (giant circular ocean surface currents). The calm waters at the centre are called the Sargasso Sea. Many animals, such as turtles, travel across the Atlantic in the Gulf Stream. The South Equatorial current flows south when it meets the coast of America. Similar circular currents are found in the Indian and Pacific oceans. There are also ocean currents that flow deep beneath the surface. Driven partly by cold,

ARCTIC OCEAN

LABRADOR CURRENT

NORTH ATLANTIC DRIFT

GULF STREAM

Sargasso Sea

Gulf of Mexico

NORTH EQUATORIAL CURRENT

GUINEA CURRENT

NORTH EQUATORIAL CURRENT

SOUTH EQUATORIAL CURRENT

...ORIAL COUNTERCURRENT

PACIFIC OCEAN

PERU CURRENT

BRAZIL CURRENT

ATLANTIC OCEAN

BENGUELA CURRENT

ANTARCTIC DRIFT

Weddell Sea

Currents carry all sorts of objects around the world. Shipwrecked sailors would send messages in bottles. Animals, like these goose barnacles clinging to the bottle, often hitch rides and become established in new areas.

Lines in the ocean

Convergences are where different currents come together, usually causing water to sink. Areas where currents part, allowing water to rise, are called divergences. In both areas, floating material, including logs, seaweed, rubbish, and even wrecks, often gathers in long lines. This attracts huge concentrations of animals and birds. In the Atlantic, baby turtles live in the floating sargassum weed and are carried out across the ocean.

dense, sinking water, they are usually much slower than surface currents. The two main masses of cold water are the Weddell Sea in the south and the seas around Norway and Greenland in the north. These sink and the cold water flows towards the equator along the bottom, gradually welling upward and becoming part of the surface currents.

OCEAN WEATHER

The weather at sea is very important, sometimes a matter of life or death. Apart from cyclones, tropical oceans have the lightest winds, particularly in the 'doldrums' on the equator. North and south of the equator, the trade winds dominate. They blow from the northeast in the northern hemisphere and from the southeast in the southern hemisphere. On either side of these are westerlies. The 'roaring forties' are westerlies that roar around the Southern Ocean. At the southern tip of South America, they are funnelled through the shallow gap between Cape Horn and the South Shetland Islands, making these among the roughest waters in the world.

Tropical cyclones form over warm water, as warm, moist air rises. They generally move westward across the oceans.

The water cycle

There is a continuous cycle of water between the oceans and the land. Water evaporates and forms clouds, which condense as rain. Water on land flows back to the sea mainly through rivers.

CLOUD GROWTH

CONDENSATION

EVAPORATION

RAIN

SURFACE RUNOFF

OCEAN

UNDERGROUND WATER

The violent hurricane

TROPICAL cyclones can reach 560–800 kilometres in diameter, and move at 6–8 metres per second. They cause greatest damage in the Caribbean, Madagascar, southern Asia and the eastern coast of Australia. They destroy coastal towns and villages and underwater life. Walls of dense cloud form rings around the centre of the 'eye' as warm, moist air is drawn in and spirals rapidly upward. The eye itself is a relatively calm area of cool, descending air.

Tropical cyclones are called hurricanes in the Atlantic and Caribbean, typhoons in the northwest Pacific, and cyclones in the Indian Ocean. Atlantic hurricanes are given names that work through the alphabet: examples are Hurricane Gilbert and Hurricane Hugo.

Record breakers

Built for speed, the tea- and wool-carrying clipper ships of the 19th century made good use of the trade winds in their journeys between Europe and the Far East and Australia. The record was 59 days between Melbourne and England. With the opening of the Suez Canal, steamships became a more reliable method of carrying cargo around the world and the clippers gradually died out.

Giant waves

The largest wave ever recorded was 34 metres high. In general, the biggest waves are found around the Alguhas Current, off southern Africa. Exceptionally high 'freak' waves may be preceded by an equally deep trough or 'hole'. Ships have been known to disappear in these.

FORCE 12

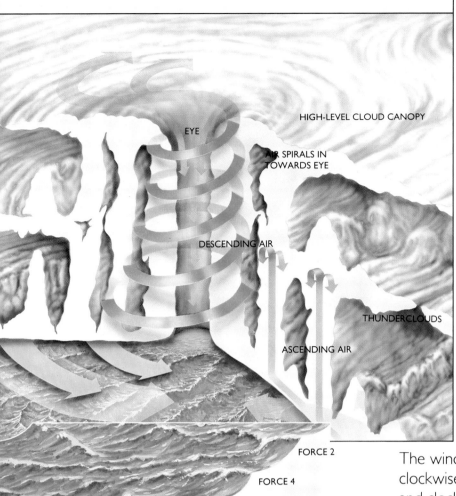

Monsoons occur mainly in the northern Indian Ocean, the China seas and the northwestern Pacific. In summer, the land becomes hotter than the sea, and the wind blows from the ocean, usually accompanied by torrential rain. In winter, the reverse occurs.

DID YOU KNOW?

The word 'ocean' comes from the Greek word 'okeanos' meaning river. The early Greeks thought a river encircled the Earth.

Waterspouts are whirling masses of air, similar to tornadoes. They usually form over warm waters, when rising, warm, moist air meets cold, dry air. Immensely destructive, waterspouts can move at several metres per second and last up to 30 minutes. 'Rains of fishes' appear if shoals are sucked up and then dropped further on.

HIGH-LEVEL CLOUD CANOPY

EYE

AIR SPIRALS IN TOWARDS EYE

DESCENDING AIR

THUNDERCLOUDS

ASCENDING AIR

FORCE 2

FORCE 4

FORCE 6

FORCE 8

FORCE 10

0 calm; sea like a mirror
1 light air; slight ripples
2 light breeze; small wavelets
3 gentle breeze; wave crests start to break
4 moderate breeze; small waves and some white horses
5 fresh breeze; frequent waves and many white horses
6 strong breeze; large waves 3 m high start
7 near gale; rough sea with spray
8 gale; waves up to 6 m high
9 strong gale; very high (up to 9 m) rough waves with much spray
10 storm; visibility difficult; waves up to 12 m high
11 violent storm; sea covered with foam, small ships lost to view between wave crests
12 hurricane; waves 14 m high and over; air filled with foam and spray.

The winds in cyclones blow anti-clockwise in the northern hemisphere and clockwise in the southern, and are always accompanied by torrential downpours of rain.

Most waves at sea are caused by the action of the wind on the surface. The distance from one crest to another can be over 300 metres and they can move at up to 95 km/h. By the time they reach land, they have lost a lot of energy and are smaller. Sometimes they flatten out to form swell.

How strong a gale?

The Beaufort Scale is used to describe the strength of the wind at sea. It is named for Francis Beaufort, an admiral in the British Navy in 1805. Although more scientific methods are now used to measure the force of the wind, this system, which relies on signs that can be seen with the eye, is still a valuable warning of stormy seas.

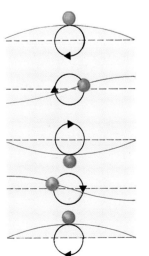

Wave energy

Perhaps surprisingly, water does not actually move forward with a wave. The water particles move in circles in one place; at the end of a wave the particles are back where they started. Only the energy that this generates moves forward with the wave.

Tidal ranges

SPRING　　　　　　　　　　　**NEAP**

THE Sun and Moon exert a strong pull on the oceans and cause the tides. The Moon pulls more than the Sun and the tides usually follow the cycle of the Moon. When the Sun and Moon are in line with each other and the Earth, the pull is greatest and tidal range is greatest; these are spring tides. When the Sun and Moon are at right angles to each other, the pull is weakest and the tidal range is small; these are neap tides.

LOW TIDE　　　HIGH TIDE　　　LOW TIDE

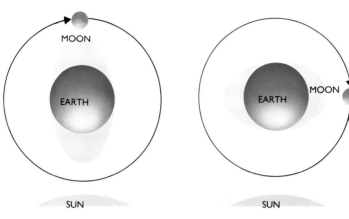

Tidal range is the difference in height between high and low tides. The largest tidal ranges are found in bays and estuaries. On open coasts the tidal range is usually between two and three metres. Enclosed seas, such as the Mediterranean, are almost tideless.

Tidal flows and cycles are very complex, and are affected by friction against the seafloor, the presence of land masses, and the shape of ocean basins. A diurnal tidal cycle is where there is just one high tide and one low tide a day, as in the Caribbean. On most

Turtles get rid of excess salt through special glands. The secretions look like tears.

When a tide turns, the opposing currents meet and may create a whirlpool (*below*). One of the most violent is the maelstrom, that forms in the Lofoten Islands off northern Norway.

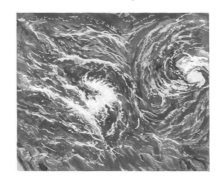

Salty seas

The open ocean has on average 35 parts of salt per 1,000 parts of seawater. The Red Sea is saltier (about 41 parts per 1,000) because few rivers flow into it to dilute it, and there is high evaporation in hot climates. Polar oceans are less salty because of melting glaciers.

Ice at sea

About 12,000–15,000 icebergs are produced each year in the Arctic, most of them having broken off from Greenland glaciers. They tend to have a conical shape and often contain debris. Antarctic icebergs, on the other hand, such as the one illustrated here, break off from the ice shelf and so are often flat-topped. Tens of thousands form each year and they are much whiter than

Changes in temperature

Temperature in the ocean varies with depth (*right*). In the tropics there is often an abrupt temperature change, or thermocline, at around 300 metres. Deep cold waters cannot mix with the warm upper layers. Towards the poles, the temperatures of these layers are similar and there is no thermocline.

SECTION THROUGH IN

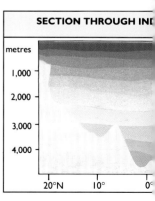

metres		
1,000		
2,000		
3,000		
4,000		

20°N　　10°　　0°

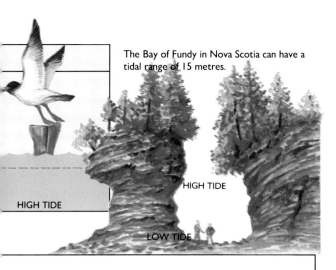

The Bay of Fundy in Nova Scotia can have a tidal range of 15 metres.

HIGH TIDE

HIGH TIDE

LOW TIDE

Arctic icebergs. About 90 per cent of an iceberg is underwater; the upper part can be over 60 metres high and several kilometres long.

Pack ice forms when the sea freezes. It is a major hindrance to ships. Waves and swell beneath it cause the ice to crack constantly and form floes that bump into each other, refreezing with hummocks and ridges. Usually a few channels remain open.

Atlantic coasts, there are two high and low tides and this is called a semi-diurnal tidal cycle. In parts of the Pacific and Indian oceans, tidal cycles are even more complex and are called 'mixed'.

The temperature of the ocean varies with depth and with latitude. In the Persian Gulf, where the sea is very shallow, temperatures can rise to 40°C. The surface waters become progressively cooler as you move away from the equator (24–30°C), to the polar oceans (0–4°C). In deeper waters, the temperature is usually very constant and is less than 4°C. Even in warm tropical waters, there are polar currents at 900 metres deep.

Seawater contains almost every chemical element. Some, vital to animal and plant life, occur in quite large quantities, such as sulphur, magnesium, calcium, and potassium. Iodine, which is essential to all living organisms, is concentrated in large amounts in seaweeds. There is even gold in seawater but probably not enough to make anyone rich.

ANTARCTICA

Why is the sea blue?

AS you can see when light is shone through a prism, light is made up of an array of colours. Red, orange, and yellow light are absorbed more quickly than blue light, which can penetrate below a 30-metre depth. This is why clean, clear mid-ocean water looks blue on sunny days. In coastal and polar waters, the plentiful animal and plant life, as well as sediments fed by the rivers, absorb more blue light, giving the water a greenish colour. This is why the colour of the southern oceans around Antarctica (*left*) is green.

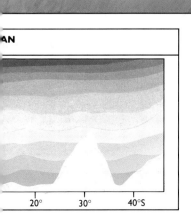

AN

20°   30°   40°S

The stranded whales
Animals, like ships, can become trapped by pack ice. In 1989 three grey whales were stranded off Alaska. People tried to help them to escape to open water by punching holes in the ice so that they could come up to breathe. Two were eventually saved.

13

OCEAN LEGENDS

Jason and the Argonauts

Jason, the nephew of the Greek king Pelias, had to sail to the kingdom of Colchis to retrieve the Golden Fleece in order to inherit the crown. At that time, the only sailing vessels were small boats or dugout canoes. Jason, therefore, asked the giant, Argus, to build him a boat large enough for 50 men. Named the *Argo*, it was an enormous craft for its time. The 50 heroes and demigods who went with Jason were called the Argonauts. The Fleece was retrieved after a hazardous journey, and on his return Jason dedicated the *Argo* to Neptune.

Lost city of Atlantis

Atlantis was a large island or continent inhabited by warlike people who attacked Mediterranean countries. In a night of floods and earthquakes it entirely disappeared beneath the sea. Numerous places have been suggested as the lost Atlantis including Santorini, a Greek, volcanic island that suffered a massive volcanic eruption thousands of years ago.

FEAR of the dangerous oceans and their cold black depths has led to widespread beliefs in sea monsters, strange beings, and supernatural phenomena at sea. These fears were compounded by the fact that little of the sea had been explored. The apparent strangeness of unfamiliar creatures brought from the depths by fishermen further fired the imagination of storytellers. Many of the stories of sea monsters are based on elements of truth. Similarly, legends of continents, such as Atlantis, lost beneath the oceans, may be based on actual places that were destroyed by real catastrophic events.

King of the sea

Neptune, who was also known as Poseidon, was the brother of Zeus, the head of the Greek gods. Neptune was king of the sea and lived in a golden palace on the seabed. He is usually shown driving over the sea in his horse-drawn chariot carrying a trident and surrounded by sea monsters. He was considered responsible for much of the weather at sea. His sons were the tritons – creatures with human bodies and fishlike tails.

Marie Celeste

The *Marie Celeste* was a 30-metre brig that set sail from New York in 1872 bound for Genoa with a cargo of industrial alcohol. One month later it was found drifting northeast of the Azores with only its storm sails hoisted. The captain had marked the brig's last position on the chart before leaving the boat, revealing the fact that it had sailed 965 kilometres alone before being found. The world's press invented numerous stories about what had happened to the crew, and it was widely but wrongly believed that when the brig was found the galley stove was still warm and there were the remains of a half-eaten meal on the captain's table. The *Marie Celeste* was finally wrecked on a reef off Haiti, some thirteen years later.

The kraken monster

Sea monsters are generally associated with bad luck and were often thought to be the cause of bad weather and other dangerous events at sea. The kraken was a huge monster that supposedly arose from the ocean depths to wrap its tentacles around ships. It is almost certainly based on sightings of the giant squid that can reach an immense size. In 1931 a specimen of 20 metres in length was found. The giant Pacific octopus is probably the origin of the legendary 'devilfish'. It can reach a length of 6 metres. It is docile and feeds mainly on crabs but shoots out of the water to grab birds.

The Bermuda Triangle

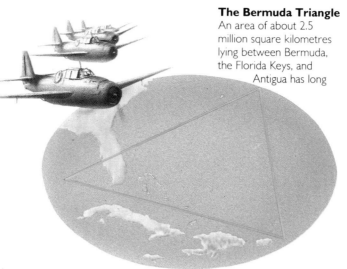

An area of about 2.5 million square kilometres lying between Bermuda, the Florida Keys, and Antigua has long been thought to have mysterious properties. It is called the Bermuda Triangle and is supposed to have claimed at least 30 aircraft and 50 ships. Explanations for these disappearances include witchcraft, reverse gravity fields, time warps, and even black holes. However, most of the losses were probably due to bad weather and hurricanes. It is now thought that the famous case of the lost squadron of U.S. Navy bombers was caused by a navigational error and that they all perished due to lack of fuel.

Moby Dick

Moby Dick is the most famous whale in literature. He was the creation of the American writer Herman Melville whose best known novel, called *Moby Dick*, was published in 1851. The story tells of how Captain Ahab pursues Moby Dick in his whaling boat, the *Pequod*, throughout the oceans after Moby Dick had attacked him on several occasions. Moby Dick is a "great white whale" (in fact a sperm whale) and Melville describes him as one of the greatest creatures of the sea. Moby Dick eludes capture and in the end capsizes the *Pequod*.

Mermaids

Mermaids were specifically thought to be part fish and part human. In northern countries seals were almost certainly behind the idea of mermaids. In the southern seas mermaids and mermen are considered to have white skin and to spend their time weaving. The origin of this may have been sightings of pale dugongs in sea-grass beds.

Pirates

Pirates, or robbers of the high seas, terrorized the Mediterranean at the time of the Greeks and Romans. Famous fictional pirates, such as Long John Silver from *Treasure Island*, are based on pirates in the Caribbean of the 17th and 18th centuries. Piracy is still a problem today around some isolated islands in Southeast Asia.

THE OCEAN FLOOR

THE ocean has an average depth of 2.9 kilometres but there are underwater chasms deeper than the highest mountains on land. Most of the seafloor consists of flat plains and rolling hills, sometimes broken by mountain ridges several kilometres high and volcanic mountains that break the surface as islands. The complexity of the seafloor is largely explained by the fact that the Earth's crust consists of plates that move over the hot mantle material that lies beneath it.

The edges of the Atlantic and Pacific oceans are different from one another. Most of the Atlantic, and much of the Indian Ocean, has a wide continental slope with many valleys, and a pronounced continental rise. The Pacific has a mainly narrow continental shelf, 19–39 kilometres wide, with a steep continental slope dropping to an ocean trench, where earthquakes often occur.

Seafloor sediments
Much of the seabed is made of sands or gravels, called oozes, which were deposited thousands of years ago by rivers or coastal erosion, and from the skeletal remains of marine animals and plants. The Atlantic receives huge quantities of sediments from rivers like the Amazon, Congo, and Niger, and the oozes are up to 500 metres thick.

NEWFOUNDLAND

UNITED STATES

CONTINENTAL SHELF

CONTINENTAL SLOPE

CONTINENTAL RISE

MID-ATLANTIC RIDGE

PUERTO RICAN TRENCH

CUBA

PUERTO RICO

JAMAICA

HISPANIOLA

The ocean shoulders
The continental shelf is a comparatively shallow extension of the land, sloping to a depth of about 200 metres. It is the part of the ocean in which most life is found. Falling off from the shelf to the ocean floor is the continental slope. The gradient is most gentle seaward of deltas, where large amounts of sediment pour out. The continental rise is formed at the bottom of the slope by all the sediment that rolls down.

Plate boundaries
Ocean trenches are long, narrow, very deep valleys found near the edge of continents or close to island chains. They are also called 'subduction zones' and are formed where one plate slides under another. Ocean ridges are long ranges rising 0.8–4 kilometres above the seafloor. They are formed where two plates pull apart and new seafloor wells up at the ridge crest and spreads away on either side.

Exploring the deep

Much of the seafloor is still a mystery to us and has never been explored. We can get some information about it from the surface, using echo sounding and other techniques, but the most exciting discoveries have been made by manned submersibles. *Alvin* is a U.S. Navy submersible which can carry two people to depths of about 4,000 metres. It has been used to photograph the extraordinary animal communities that live around thermal vents.

Creatures of the vents

Thermal vents are like 'oases' in the deep oceans. While much of the deep seabed is like a 'desert' with little or no life, a wide variety of strange animals cluster around the hot springs. They occur mainly near the ocean ridges and release sulphur-rich hot water through high chimneys, known as 'smokers'. Worms up to 10 centimetres long and 3 metres in diameter have been found living in intertwined white tubes. There are also clams 25 centimetres long, strange limpets, crabs, sea anemones, and some fish. These animals do not need sunlight, and there are no plants for them to eat, but they make their own food, using sulphur and bacteria. Each vent may last only about 100 years, but new ones seem to form as old ones disappear.

ABYSSAL PLAIN

AFRICA

Undersea plains

The abyssal plains are among the flattest places on Earth. They are formed by the sediments which rain down from the ocean surface or pour down the continental slope, smoothing the contours of the ocean crust. The Indian and Atlantic Oceans have more abyssal plains than the Pacific as they receive more sediment.

Volcanic islands

Oceanic islands are formed by volcanoes which break the ocean surface. Some are grouped in chains and linked by submarine ridges of lava. Although many volcanoes do not reach the ocean surface, some, like Mauna Loa, one of the Hawaiian islands in the Pacific, are higher than Mount Everest.

The continents and ocean basins are not fixed into position on the Earth. Although we cannot feel it, they are constantly moving at speeds of just a few centimetres a year. The way in which the surface of the Earth moves has been worked out in the theory of plate tectonics.

The rigid outer layer of the Earth, called the lithosphere, varies in thickness from a few to 240 kilometres and is broken into six main plates. The energy produced by heat in the deep inner part of the Earth makes the plates move over the hot, molten inner layer (the asthenosphere). The outer part of the lithosphere is called the crust.

Continental movements

THE continents of today bear little resemblance to those of 400 million years ago, when in a series of giant collisions, the separate continents welded together into a single, huge supercontinent – Pangaea.

Around 160 million years ago, huge thermal upwellings in the underlying mantle dragged at the Earth's crust and Pangaea broke into two main blocks: Gondwana in the south and Laurasia in the north. Gondwana consisted of modern South America, Africa, India, Australia, and perhaps, Antarctica; Laurasia was made up of what is now North America, Europe, and Asia. They were separated by the Tethys Ocean. About 100 million years ago, the Atlantic started to form as the African and South American plates moved apart, and Laurasia split into two. The Tethys Ocean was closed as India separated and moved north about 80 million years ago. The breakup of Gondwana was complete when Australia broke off Antarctica about 40 million years ago. The coastlines of

TODAY

the continents today can be fitted together like a jigsaw to show how they were originally joined up. The plates are still moving. North America is moving away from Europe at a rate of about 8 cm a year.

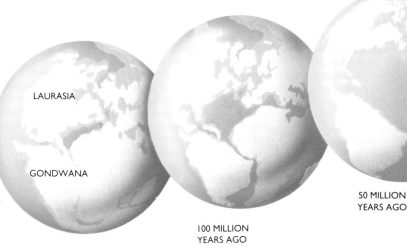

LAURASIA

GONDWANA

160 MILLION YEARS AGO

100 MILLION YEARS AGO

50 MILLION YEARS AGO

Shaping the ocean floor

WHERE two plates are being pushed apart, the hot material from the inner mantle rises to fill the space and form a new seafloor. Oceanic ridges form along these lines. The Pacific and Nazca plates that make up the Pacific floor are being pushed apart at the fastest rate of all plates, by about 14 centimetres a year.

Where two plates are colliding, one is forced under the other and down into the mantle. This is called a subduction zone and it is here that ocean trenches are formed. These areas are usually seismic, with a high likelihood of earthquakes. Earthquakes are also common where two plates grind past each other, as is happening at the San Andreas Fault along the western coast of North America.

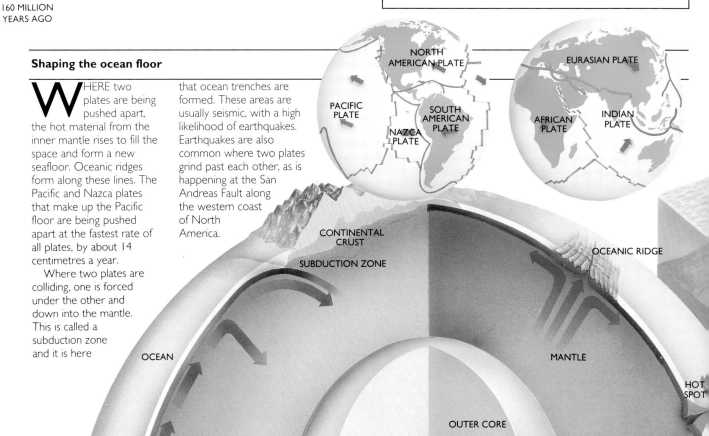

Birth of an ocean

THE Red Sea may one day become an ocean. The African and Arabian plates started moving apart 70 million years ago, and are still

doing so by about half a centimetre a year. This movement probably created the Great Rift Valley, a gash in the continental crust that runs from the Jordan Valley and Dead Sea in the north down through East Africa in the south. When this valley broke through it linked the Red Sea to the Mediterranean.

This link has been broken and rejoined several times. Once the Red Sea was connected naturally to the Mediterranean and Indian Ocean.

RED SEA

OCEANIC RIDGE

How islands are formed

SOME islands are formed from bits of granite crust that have broken off a continent and been left behind, such as the Seychelles that were part of Gondwana 100

Hot spots are where plumes of magma rise to the surface from the mantle. The hot spot is stationary and a chain of volcanoes is formed as the plate moves over it.

MIDWAY

HAWAIIAN ARCHIPELAGO

million years ago. Others are formed by volcanic eruptions on oceanic ridges, along subduction zones, or over hot spots.

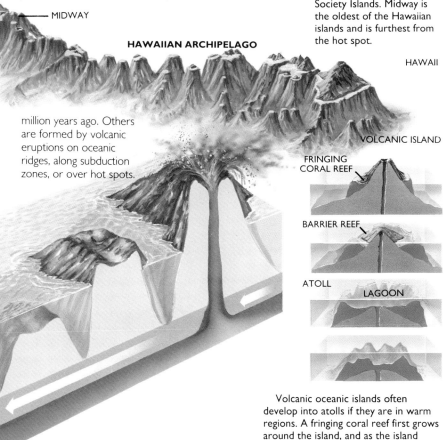

Oceanic crust that forms the bottoms of the ocean basins is made of basalt. Continental crust is made of granite that is less dense than basalt, and so sits on top. Oceans form, grow, shrink, or disappear depending on the relative movements of these plates. The Atlantic Ocean, for example, has probably widened by about 15 metres in the last 500 years.

Death of an ocean

The Tethys Ocean was squeezed out when the Indian plate collided with, and was subducted under, the Eurasian plate. When the continental crust of India met that of Asia it buckled up and the Himalayas were formed. Parts of the shallow continental shelf of the Tethys Ocean were lifted in the process so that marine shells can now be found thousands of metres up in the Himalayas.

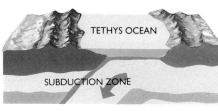

TETHYS OCEAN

SUBDUCTION ZONE

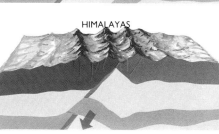

HIMALAYAS

Sixteen hot spots are known, including the Hawaiian archipelago and Society Islands. Midway is the oldest of the Hawaiian islands and is furthest from the hot spot.

HAWAII

VOLCANIC ISLAND

FRINGING CORAL REEF

BARRIER REEF

ATOLL

LAGOON

Volcanic oceanic islands often develop into atolls if they are in warm regions. A fringing coral reef first grows around the island, and as the island sinks the reef keeps growing. Eventually the central island may disappear leaving a lagoon surrounded by a coral reef.

DID YOU KNOW?

Tidal waves have little connection with tides. They are usually caused by undersea volcanic eruptions or earthquakes that cause mass water movements and large waves.

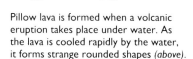

Pillow lava is formed when a volcanic eruption takes place under water. As the lava is cooled rapidly by the water, it forms strange rounded shapes (above).

Islands often have unique animals and plants. Continental islands have species that may be strange descendants of those that existed on the mainland thousands of years ago, such as the sea coconut of the Seychelles (below). Species can only reach oceanic islands by wind, ocean currents, on objects such as floating logs, or by people.

SEA COCONUT

Submarines

On the ocean surface, a submarine's ballast tanks are full of air. When it dives, the valves on these tanks are opened, air rushes out, and water floods in through the ports in the bottom. To surface, high-pressure air is released into the tops of the tanks and the water is forced out (see diagram below). Conventional submarines use diesel engines when running just below the surface and battery power at greater depths.

A nuclear-powered submarine can operate for months without refuelling. Oxygen and fresh water are extracted from seawater for the crew. The world's first nuclear-powered submarine, the USS Nautilus, built in 1954, achieved fame when it crossed the North Pole under the ice.

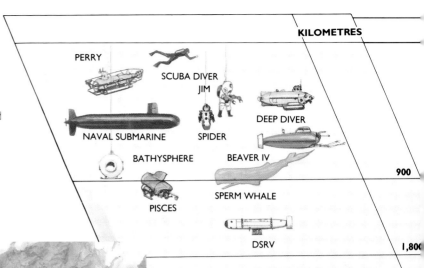

KILOMETRES

PERRY
SCUBA DIVER
JIM
DEEP DIVER
NAVAL SUBMARINE
SPIDER
BATHYSPHERE
BEAVER IV
PISCES
SPERM WHALE
DSRV
900
1,800

DIVING SAUCER

WRECK OF TITANIC
ALVIN

FNRS-3

JASON

SURFACE CRUISING
DIVING
SUBMERGED CRUISING
SURFACING

Over 98 per cent of the seabed is still unexplored, but in recent years enormous progress has been made in developing methods for studying the oceans. Research vessels still play an important role. Much can be learned by towing instruments behind ships, collecting samples in nets, and bringing material up from the seabed. Offshore buoys relay information by radio, and satellites can transmit readings, such as temperature, ice cover, and wave height, back to Earth.

Small, manoeuvrable submersibles are best suited for research and industrial purposes, and the needs of the offshore oil industry have stimulated their development. Jacques Cousteau

The voyages of Challenger

Between 1872 and 1876 the ship Challenger made deep-sea investigations at over 300 spots in all the oceans. Depth soundings were made and samples of sediment and water and specimens of plants and animals and temperature readings were taken. The equipment used by Challenger would seem very old-fashioned to modern oceanographers, but the information it gathered provided the basis for much of our knowledge about the sea.

Deep-sea diving

IDEALLY, undersea craft should have a strong hull to withstand pressure, a means of controlling buoyancy and depth, and a propulsion system.

The bathysphere was a heavy steel sphere that could be lowered from a ship's cable. In the 1930s it reached what were then record levels of around 900 metres. A bathyscaphe, such as *FNRS-3*, had a motor, used petrol for buoyancy, and jettisoned iron shot when it needed to surface. In 1960 the three-person bathyscaphe *Trieste* managed to reach the bottom of the Challenger Deep, at 11,300 metres, the deepest point in the sea.

Submersibles, such as *Beaver IV*, are built of very light material for buoyancy. *Pisces* is a commercial submersible that can go to 2,000 metres. Some, such as *Perry* and *Deep Diver*, have a 'lock-out chamber' through which divers can leave to explore.

Jason is an ROV that explores wrecks with the help of remotely operated video cameras. The crewed DSRV, or Deep Submergence Rescue Vehicle, is used to rescue sunken submarine crews.

built the first submersible, the *Soucoupe Plongeante* (diving saucer), in 1959. Submersibles consist of a pressure-proof hull, viewing ports, external lights, and a variety of manipulators, cameras, and other gadgets. Equally useful are underwater robots or ROVs (Remotely Operated Vehicles) that are usually tethered to ships from which control signals are relayed. Submersibles and ROVs are used for pipe laying, repair work, taking photos, collecting samples, launching divers at depth, and many other deep-water operations.

Diving suits

RIGID suits, such as *Spider* (below) and *Jim* (see *chart*, *centre*), are like mini-submersibles and enable divers to go deeper by keeping them at surface pressure. *Spider* has its own air supply and moves with propellers driven by electric motors.

IN the 17th century, people went underwater using diving bells, and it was not until the 19th century that the 'hard-hat' suit was invented. This consisted of a copper helmet and weighted boots, with air supplied from the surface. In 1943 diving was revolutionized when French marine explorer Jacques Cousteau and engineer Emile Gagnan invented SCUBA gear (Self-Contained Underwater Breathing Apparatus). Compressed air is supplied from a tank on the diver's back. Commercial divers have all sorts of gadgets to make their work easier; their suits can be heated and they use battery operated scooters to get around more quickly.

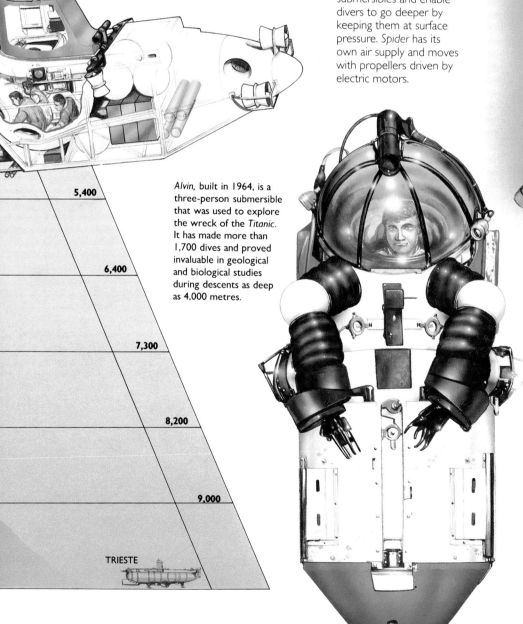

5,400

6,400

7,300

8,200

9,000

Alvin, built in 1964, is a three-person submersible that was used to explore the wreck of the *Titanic*. It has made more than 1,700 dives and proved invaluable in geological and biological studies during descents as deep as 4,000 metres.

TRIESTE

THE LIVING OCEANS

THE sea is an ideal environment for plant and animal life. It allows light to penetrate and there is abundant oxygen and many of the vital chemicals and compounds necessary for life. Its high density enables animals to float, so the largest animals on Earth have been able to live here.

Most sea life is found along coasts and in the surface waters where there is more light and food. 'Pelagic' animals are those that live in the water itself. They may drift in ocean currents, like plankton, or swim, like whales. 'Benthic' animals live on the sea bottom. Many, such as corals, live attached to the seabed or to other hard objects. Others live buried in sediments, like worms, or are more active and hunt, like lobsters.

Indian Ocean life
The Indian Ocean has many animals in common with the Pacific because they have been linked for a long time. The Red Sea, in contrast, has some unique species, including some reef fish, as it has been separated from the Indian Ocean. Much of the Indian Ocean is now a sanctuary for whales.

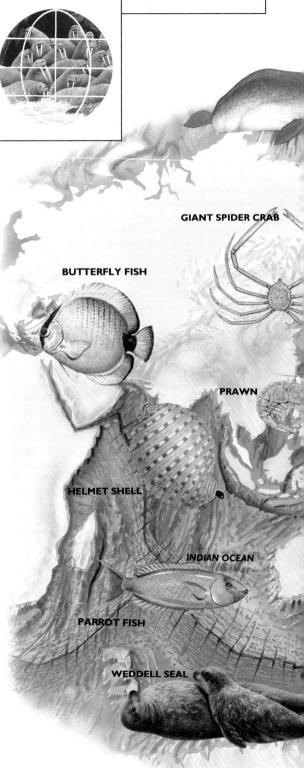

GIANT SPIDER CRAB

BUTTERFLY FISH

PRAWN

HELMET SHELL

INDIAN OCEAN

PARROT FISH

WEDDELL SEAL

SEA LETTUCE

KELP

BLADDER WRACK

CORALLINA

Marine plants
Although they are microscopic in size, the phytoplankton that floats in surface waters makes up about 90 per cent of ocean plants. The others are the much larger nonflowering seaweeds (or algae) and the only flowering plants that can grow in seawater, the sea grasses.

Seaweeds are classified by their colour: Brown and most green seaweeds need direct sunlight and live in shallow waters. Many of the reds and a few greens need only a little light and are found deeper or in caves. Like land plants, seaweeds are often seasonal, growing in great abundance in the spring and summer and dying off in the winter. Many seaweeds have a jelly-like texture and some have limy skeletons and look like rocks.

Antarctic life
The Southern or Antarctic Ocean has enormous numbers of marine animals that live on the abundant plankton, such as the tiny krill. Huge colonies of penguins, albatrosses, and seals are found on Antarctic shores.

Arctic life
Arctic animals are adapted to life on floating pack ice, and long cold winters. Large mammals such as the narwhal, polar bear, and seals take advantage of the abundant fish. Auks are the northern equivalent of penguins.

Atlantic life
The Atlantic has a smaller number of species than the Pacific but they are just as varied. Warm-water species like sea turtles are found in the Caribbean. Squid fishing is a major industry around the Falkland Islands. The Mediterranean has several unique plants and animals such as the beautiful and precious red coral.

NARWHAL

ARCTIC OCEAN

POLAR BEAR

AUK

COMMON DOLPHIN

BEARDED SEAL

GIANT OCTOPUS

MANATEE

RED CORAL

GIANT CLAM

MARINE IGUANA

PACIFIC OCEAN

WHITE PELICAN

GREAT WHITE SHARK

SQUID

PENGUIN

ATLANTIC OCEAN

ANGLERFISH

ALBATROSS

Albatrosses have enormous wings, enabling them to glide for hour after hour over the southern seas. The wandering albatross has a wingspan of 3.7 metres.

Pacific life
Animals of the Pacific range from the giant spider crab and giant octopus found in the north, to the giant clams and varied fish life found on coral reefs around atolls. Pacific islanders depend on many of the fish, molluscs, and crustaceans in these waters for food.

23

EARLIEST LIFE

It was in the ancient seas, rather than on land, that life first formed about 3,500 million years ago. One of the earliest forms of life was a microscopic organism similar to a plant that made its food using energy from sunlight and hydrogen from water. Its living descendants are known as 'blue-greens' or cyanobacteria. Some blue-greens secrete lime and form stony cushions called stromatolites. Fossil stromatolites are found in many places; the oldest ones, and thus the oldest known life on Earth, are at a place called North Pole in Australia. Living ones still survive in a few places such as Shark Bay in Western Australia. The blue-greens were important because in removing hydrogen from water, they released oxygen. Gradually the concentration of oxygen in the atmosphere increased, giving us the air on which we now depend.

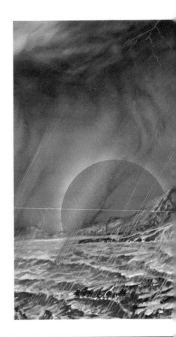

After the Earth condensed from the mass of gas and dust swirling in space, gases such as water vapour emerged from the Earth in volcanic eruptions. Water from volcanoes and rain from the sky formed ponds that gradually expanded and joined to form the first oceans and seas, four billion years ago.

Most of the Precambrian animals *(inset, right)* found in the earliest seas between 3,500 and 590 million years ago were soft-bodied and a little like our modern jellyfish, sea pens, and worms.

The first fish on land

COELACANTHS were the first fish to pull themselves out of the sea onto land and so were probably the ancestors of many land animals. Many species of coelacanth have been found as fossils but there is only one species still living today.

In 1938 a living coelacanth was caught off South Africa. This caused immense excitement, and since then about 200 more have been caught, mainly from around the Comoros Islands in the Indian Ocean. So many people have been trying to catch coelacanths to put on display it is feared the species could become extinct. However, it is now protected. Fortunately, the modern coelacanth lives in deep waters and unlike its fossil ancestors never tries to come on land, where it would almost certainly meet an unhappy end at the hands of collectors.

Early seabirds
Seabirds looking much like some of those found today were living about 70 million years ago in the shallow seas that covered much of what is now North America. *Hesperornis* was flightless but swam by kicking its large webbed feet and could chase fast-moving fish underwater, catching them in its toothed beak.

HESPERORNIS

ICHTHYOSAUR

PLESIOSAUR

COELACANTH FOSSIL

Dinosaurs of the sea
The true dinosaurs all lived on land but some groups of prehistoric reptiles living about 200 million years ago took to the sea. Ichthyosaurs had dolphin-shaped bodies and plesiosaurs had long necks that were useful for catching fish. Plesiosaurs could be nearly 15 metres long and were able to come onto land on their four paddle-shaped limbs. The limbs of both ichthyosaurs and plesiosaurs were adapted as paddles for swimming and both reptiles fed on fish and squid.

Burgess shale fossils

ALTHOUGH there is a poor fossil record for most of the ancient seas, fossils were found in 1909 at Burgess Pass in British Columbia, Canada. The outcrop of shale there is formed from compressed muds laid down on the ocean edge almost 550 million years ago. Within it are preserved a variety of life forms which existed then. These fossils are some of the most perfectly preserved in the world. Many of the forms found as fossils have descendants we can recognize now, a few billion generations later, on modern beaches and sea floors, or swimming in the oceans. These include sea urchins, jellyfish, starfish, and worms.

Ammonites and trilobites

Ammonite shells were divided into air-filled compartments that made them buoyant. Some species were as big as truck wheels yet may still have been almost weightless in the water. Their only living descendant is the pearly nautilus. Trilobites had protective shells and could roll up into a ball. The only similar modern animal is the horseshoe crab.

Grand Canyon fossils

As seas have risen and fallen, and new land masses have formed, so fossils of ancient sea creatures have come to lie far inland. At the Grand Canyon in North America, the Colorado River has cut through layers of sediments that were once the bottoms of seas. About halfway down the Canyon's sides, there are 400-million-year-old fish fossils. Farther down, there are 500-million-year-old shells and worms .

The ancient seas contained more types of animal than we will ever know because many of them were largely soft-bodied and have not been preserved as fossils. About 570 million years ago there was a huge explosion of marine life, ammonites, and trilobites. However, they and hundreds of other marine species, died out inexplicably between 100 and 65 million years ago, at the same time as the dinosaurs.

Fossils form much more easily in the sea than on land because sediments are constantly laid down rather than eroded away. Dead organisms are rapidly covered and preserved.

AMMONITE

TRILOBITE

LEVELS OF OCEAN LIFE

The ocean food cycle
During winter in the northern oceans storms and currents stir up the seabed and bring nutrients (the vital elements that living organisms need) to the surface. This, combined with the extra sunlight from longer days, causes plankton to bloom and increase rapidly during spring. Once summer is over, the plankton that is not eaten by other sea creatures dies and sinks to the bottom and the whole cycle starts again. In the southern oceans the seabed is constantly stirred up and plankton is abundant throughout most of the year. Because of the thermocline (*see page 12*) there is little stirring in the tropics except in the upwelling areas, and so there is often less plankton.

FRIGATE BIRD

GANNET

FLYING FISH

MANGROVE TREES

TOOTHED WRACK

BASKING SHARK

COCKLE

PLAICE

MINKE WHALE

GREY SEAL

KELP

COD

MUDSKIPPER

QUEEN SCALLOP

SHORE CRAB

OCTOPUS

PERIWINKLE

SAND GAPER

CONGER EEL

HERMIT CRAB IN WHELK SHELL

SEA GRASS

SEA SQUIRTS

BLUE SHARK

EAGLE RAY

SEA URCHIN

LUMP SUCKER

CUTTLEFISH

SEA CUCUMBER

BRITTLE STARS

RAT-TAIL FISHES

SEA PENS

SCALE WORM

HATCHET FISH

SEA LILY

STARFISH

CORAL

In shallow waters
The highest density of life on the seabed is found in shallow water down to about 90 metres. Plants such as sea grasses, kelp, and other seaweeds are found only here. Muddy and silty sea bottoms have a rich invertebrate life that attracts large numbers of seabirds. Sea cucumbers, starfish, and snail-like molluscs are found on sandy and muddy sea bottoms. Bottom-living fish are often well camouflaged.

Upper continental slopes
The types of animal found on the upper continental slope, down to 1,500 metres, depend on whether the seabed is rocky, muddy, or sandy. So that they do not sink, animals living on muds and oozes have spines, stalks, long legs, or hairs. Sea pens, for example, were named when people wrote with quills because they looked just like feathers. Sponges, corals, rays, and a variety of other fish are also found here.

Lower continental slopes and abyssal plains
The lower continental slope from 1,500 to 3,000 metres has few animals. These include worms, bivalves, sea cucumbers, and some fish that feed mainly on the remains of plants and animals that have fallen from the surface. Some species are entirely dependent on bacteria in the sediments. Tripod fish, found from 300 to 6,000 metres, are typical of the fish at these depths. They rest on soft oozes on their stiffened fins and tails, facing the current and trapping the rain of particles from the surface.

Similar animals are found on the abyssal plains of ooze and mud at 3,000 to 6,000 metres. The communities of animals (*see page 17*) found around hydrothermal vents are like oases in a desert and do not depend upon the complex food web that relies on surface-water phytoplankton.

Food for many

In healthy seas, phytoplankton is eaten almost as fast as it is produced. Numerous animals including jellyfish, comb jellies, shrimps (*Penaeus*), herrings, anchovies, and even huge blue and grey whales feed on both plant and animal plankton.

Animal plankton

The animal plankton or 'zooplankton' feed on the phytoplankton. Some, such as copepods and krill, spend all their lives in the ocean surface waters. Copepods are the most abundant. Other zooplankton are the young or 'larvae' of much larger marine animals such as corals and fish, many of which are eaten before they reach adulthood.

Plankton and the food web

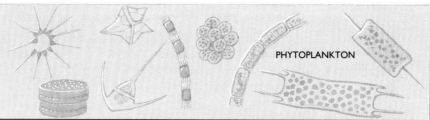

PLANKTON, the tiny plants and animals that drift in the sunlit surface waters, are at the top of the ocean food web. Most are various types of plant or 'phytoplankton' (*below*). Phytoplankton are usually found in water 30–40 metres deep. Like plants on land, these use the energy of sunlight to make food from carbon and other elements in the water, a process called photosynthesis. Diatoms are very common phytoplankton and have shells of silica. Two possible fates await all types of plankton. Either they may be eaten by larger predators, such as fish, or they may die and sink to the seabed.

PHYTOPLANKTON

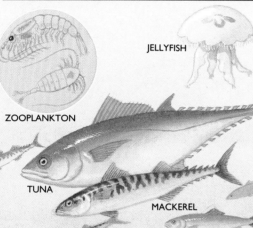

JELLYFISH

ZOOPLANKTON

TUNA

MACKEREL

HERRING

GRAY'S WHALE

OAR FISH

ANGLER FISH

OPISTHOPROCTUS SOLEATUS

SPONGES

GULPER EEL

PHOTICHTHYS ARGENTEUS

TRIPOD FISH

EEL

WORM   LINGULA

AMPHIPODS AND ISOPODS

SEA CUCUMBER

Plankton-eaters, as well as animals that feed on them, are found in both surface waters and at depths below 90 metres. They include tuna, mackerel, sharks, and squid. The food web becomes very complicated, with larger fish, seals, whales, and seabirds eating smaller fish. Whales and seals in the southern oceans may get through 10 million tonnes of squid a year. Below 180 metres there is no light, and the amount of food available drops off rapidly towards 2,000 metres. At these depths predatory fish, such as hatchet fish and bristle mouths, that eat fish, squid, and crustaceans, predominate. These predators often have huge mouths and big eyes to ensure they catch any food that appears. Many also have luminous organs to attract their prey.

Ocean trenches

Surprisingly, animals have been found in deep ocean trenches that go below 6,000 metres. Each trench has its own unique community of strange and often quite large sea cucumbers, mollusks, worms, and crustaceans.

27

INVERTEBRATES

Christmas tree worm
Many marine worms spend all their lives in tubes, catching food from the water with their feathery tentacles. Usually they can pull their tentacles back into the tube in a split second. The Christmas tree worms are brightly coloured and live in tubes buried in corals.

About 97 per cent of the animals in the world are invertebrates. These are animals without backbones or internal skeletons. They include many terrestrial animals, such as insects and spiders, but there is also a huge variety in the sea. They range in size from the tiny animals that float in the plankton to the huge giant squid, up to 20 metres long.

The main groups of marine invertebrates are very different from each other. Sponges, corals, and sea anemones are unable to move and live attached to rocks or the seabed.

Feather stars or crinoids are common in the tropics. They grip rocks or corals with their spiky 'cirri' and use their feathery arms for swimming and filtering food from the water. They are related to starfish.

Sponges

MOST people think of sponges as something you use for washing or bathing. In fact, they are marine animals – of the simplest kind. They are basically just a collection of cells surrounding a network of holes and channels through which water flows. These nooks and crannies often provide a home for other animals such as starfish and little crabs – several thousand shrimp have been found inside a single sponge! Bath sponges all have rather dull colours, but many other sponges have brilliant colours and strange shapes. Their bodies are often supported by spicules, tiny, needle-like slivers of glass which are almost invisible. The giant vase sponges (*below*) found on coral reefs can grow as high as a diver. Perhaps the most amazing thing about sponges is that new sponges can grow from tiny pieces of broken sponge.

The deadly cone shell
Cone shells, like this textile cone (*above*) have beautifully patterned shells. They can catch fish and other animals several times their size. They spear their prey with a harpoon-like tooth and paralyse it with a nerve poison before devouring it. The poison is so powerful it can even kill human beings.

Portuguese man-of-war
Jellyfish are well named – even the firmest ones are 94 per cent water. They catch food with their tentacles which are armed with stinging cells. The Portuguese man-of-war is not a true jellyfish; it is in fact a colony of similar animals that float together on the surface attached to a gas-filled sac. The tentacles can be several metres in length and are highly poisonous.

The pen shell
The pen shell is the largest Mediterranean bivalve. It is attached to the sea bottom by strong threads. In Italy the threads were once woven to make gloves.

The torpedo-shaped squid is the fastest marine invertebrate. Some species can shoot out of the water and reach speeds of up to 25 km/h. Both squid and octopus produce a dark brown ink called sepia which they squirt out to confuse predators. Some deep-sea squid are luminescent (they give out light).

Scallops
Unlike many bivalve molluscs, scallops can move very quickly. They hop across the seabed by jet propulsion, snapping their hinged shells together to shoot out a water current. They have eyes around the edge of their shells.

DID YOU KNOW?

Sea anemones and jellyfish are very closely related. The sea anemone is like an upside-down jellyfish that spends its life attached to rocks.

Sea urchins have a hard outer covering with many spines. They have a unique kind of mouth, called Aristotle's lantern, which has teeth to scrape algae off corals and rocks.

The sea mouse is actually a worm covered with silky bristles.

The Mediterranean murex produces a secretion which is colourless at first, but turns deep purple in sunlight. The Romans used this as a dye for their togas. No one knows what the murex uses it for!

The beautiful pirates

SEA slugs have no shell and are often poisonous, to protect them from predators. They are some of the most beautifully coloured of all sea invertebrates. Their bright colours serve as a warning, or act as camouflage on the colourful coral reef. The delicate, patterned tentacles on their backs are their gills. Many sea slugs float near the surface of the water and feed on anemones and jellyfish, 'pirating' the stinging cells of their prey. These are reused in the gill tufts as protection.

Marine worms are much more colourful than land worms and often have tentacles or bristles. The molluscs are the largest group, and include snail-like animals with a single shell, the bivalves with two hinged shells, and the octopus, squid, and sea slugs, most of which have lost their shells. The crustaceans have hard outer 'suits of armour' which they have to moult in order to grow. The starfish, feather stars and sea urchins belong to a group of circular or star-shaped animals.

Hermits of the sea
Hermit crabs have soft bodies and live inside mollusc shells for protection. They change the shell as they grow. Sometimes they put other animals, such as sponges or sea anemones, onto their shells to camouflage them.

Life on a whale's head
Barnacles are crustaceans that live in a shell. They wave their legs outside the shell to catch food. They spend all their lives attached to rocks, objects such as ships and harbour walls, and even living animals such as whales.

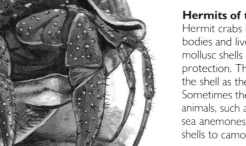

FISH

Fish include some of the ugliest and some of the most beautiful sea creatures. They range in size from large sharks to tiny colourful reef fish, but they generally have the characteristic fin and tail shape that is so well-adapted for swimming. Like marine invertebrates, they spend their entire lives underwater and obtain oxygen by passing water through their gills.

Sharks, rays, and skates have cartilaginous skeletons, and their skin is covered by tiny rough teeth called denticles.

Schools of fish

Many fish of the open sea swim together in schools, moving simultaneously in the same direction. This confuses predators, who find it difficult to follow a single individual. Schools, or shoals of fish, can be enormous. Many open-sea fish are dark on their upper parts and pale underneath. This provides camouflage from both above and below.

Hunter and hunted

THE swordfish is found in all tropical oceans but has been known to stray as far north as Iceland. The sword is in fact an elongated snout and is covered with rough tooth-like projections. It is usually a solitary hunter, using its sword to slash at shoals of fish so that it can then feed on the injured. Swordfish have been known to go right through the bottom of boats, and even pierce whales. It is not known if these are intentional attacks, or simply collisions, as they are one of the fastest creatures in the sea and can reach speeds of 240 kilometres per hour. They are a popular catch with sport fishermen.

Great white shark

THE great white shark has acquired a bad reputation as a result of the cinema, but in fact it rarely kills humans. The great white feeds mainly on seals and porpoises and is rarely over 7.5 metres in length. As in all sharks, its teeth, up to 8 centimetres long, are constantly replaced. At any one time, sharks may have up to 3,000 teeth in their mouth arranged in between six and twenty rows. Only the first couple of rows are used. The others are replacement teeth that move forward on a system very similar to a conveyor belt. Great white sharks are found in warm, but usually not tropical, seas. Most have been sighted off the coasts of California and Australia.

Some sharks are unable to keep afloat unless they swim. Many sharks also have to keep a constant stream of water passing through their gills or they will drown, so they spend most of their time swimming. A few are able to pump water through their gills: these species can lie on the sea bottom. Most fish have bony skeletons and are covered with bony scales. The bony fish have a swim bladder, or air sac, that allows them to float.

Gliders of the seas

Manta rays (*left*) are flattened relatives of sharks and are the largest of the skates and rays. The Pacific manta has a wingspan of over 7 metres and weighs up to 1,600 kg. It is one of the most majestic swimmers, gliding through the surface waters of the tropical oceans, flapping its 'wings'. Despite its size, it feeds on small fish and invertebrates that it filters out of the water. The two fins that project from its head like horns have given it the name 'devilfish'.

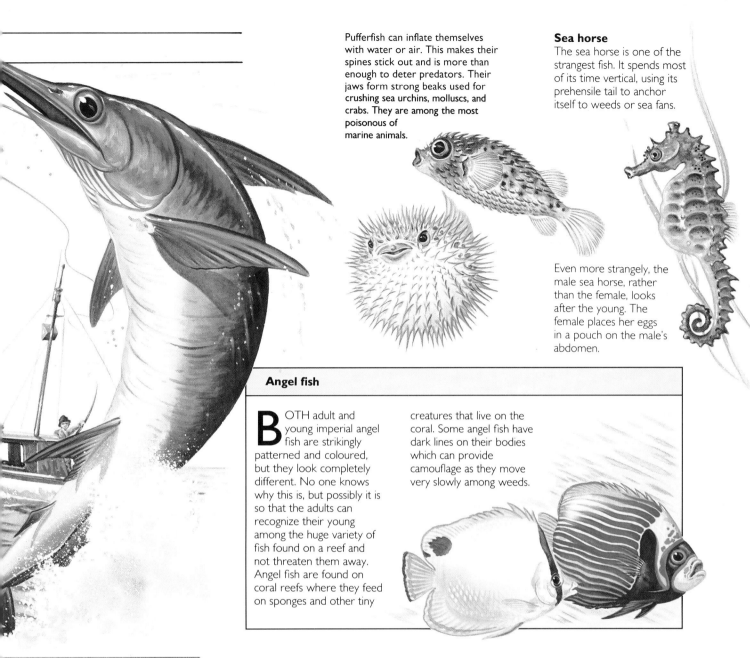

Pufferfish can inflate themselves with water or air. This makes their spines stick out and is more than enough to deter predators. Their jaws form strong beaks used for crushing sea urchins, molluscs, and crabs. They are among the most poisonous of marine animals.

Sea horse

The sea horse is one of the strangest fish. It spends most of its time vertical, using its prehensile tail to anchor itself to weeds or sea fans.

Even more strangely, the male sea horse, rather than the female, looks after the young. The female places her eggs in a pouch on the male's abdomen.

Angel fish

BOTH adult and young imperial angel fish are strikingly patterned and coloured, but they look completely different. No one knows why this is, but possibly it is so that the adults can recognize their young among the huge variety of fish found on a reef and not threaten them away. Angel fish are found on coral reefs where they feed on sponges and other tiny creatures that live on the coral. Some angel fish have dark lines on their bodies which can provide camouflage as they move very slowly among weeds.

Angler fish

Angler fish are among the ugliest of sea creatures. They are often flabby and lumpy and usually have huge mouths. They have very elastic stomachs and tend to eat anything. Their name comes from the lure on their heads, an adaptation of one of their dorsal fin rays, with a tiny, fleshy flap at the end of it. This can be moved around like a bait on a line to attract other small fish that the angler fish then eats. Deep-sea angler fish (*left*) living in dark waters have luminous lures. The light on these lures is formed by chemicals or by bacteria that glow naturally.

Flatfish

Flatfish, such as plaice, flounders, and halibut, start life as normal-shaped fish with an eye on each side of the head. As they grow, one eye moves round and the mouth twists until the adult can lie on one side.

Adults can change colour perfectly to match the pattern and colour of the seabed, thus helping to protect themselves from predators. They also often bury themselves in the sand in shallow water.

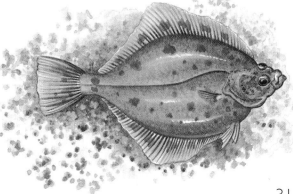

MAMMALS

Sea otter

The sea otter of the north Pacific rarely comes ashore. It digs for clams and finds food in the kelp. Apart from monkeys and humans, it is the only animal known to use a tool. It breaks open abalone and other molluscs between two stones while floating on its back. At night, it wraps itself in giant seaweed to avoid drifting out to sea. It was hunted almost to extinction but it is now protected and populations have increased.

Unlike fish, mammals and reptiles have to come to the surface of the sea to breathe air, and most must come to shore to breed and lay their eggs. Nevertheless, they are well adapted to life underwater and their bodies are designed to conserve oxygen. When diving, a seal's heartbeat may slow from about 140 beats a minute to less than 15. Mammals have a high body temperature and lose heat more rapidly in water than in air. Most marine mammals therefore have a special layer of fat, called blubber, under the skin that provides insulation. Reptiles, which are cold-blooded, must find other ways of keeping warm. Marine iguanas bask in the sun to warm up before swimming; marine turtles solve the problem by living mainly in tropical seas. The fact that they have to come ashore to breed, and are very clumsy on land, has meant that many marine mammals and reptiles are vulnerable to hunters.

Sea snakes are found in the Indian and Pacific oceans. They have very strong venom but rarely bite humans. They may be the most abundant reptiles on Earth.

A poorly adapted mammal

HUMAN beings are very poorly adapted to life underwater. The invention of scuba gear has meant that we can get some idea of what it is like to be a seal. A diver takes compressed air down to provide oxygen. A special diving suit keeps her warm. Fins make fairly good paddles, and a mask helps her to see. But we have not solved the problem of eating under water! A diver on land in all her equipment is almost as clumsy as a seal on land.

Seals in combat

Adult seals usually gather once a year to breed, sometimes thousands crowding on to one beach at the same time. The males set up territories and fight fiercely with each other. Bull elephant seals have particularly vicious fights over their females. Their strange trunk-like noses are inflated and used to threaten other males. Bulls may be three times the weight of the females . Like other true seals (those with no external ear flaps), elephant seals have great difficulty moving on land. In contrast, eared seals can turn their hind flippers forward and move fairly quickly on land. The limbs of all seals are adapted for swimming. Eared seals, such as sea lions and fur seals, swim with their front flippers. The true seals use their hind flippers for power and their front flippers to steer.

The male elephant seal's enormous nose is used as a loudspeaker to amplify the animal's threatening roars, which can be heard several kilometres away.

Walrus

The walrus lives in the Arctic. Its long tusks are modified teeth and are used to help it pull itself out on to ice floes and to show its dominance over other walruses. The largest animal with the largest tusks generally wins in fights. Walruses have very thick skins to protect themselves from injury in fights. Like seals, walruses may have problems keeping cool in hot sunshine. They often go pink in the sun, as the blood comes to the skin surface to cool down.

Sea cows

Surprisingly, dugongs and manatees are related to elephants rather than to seals. They live in shallow tropical waters, and like whales do not come ashore at all. Dugongs live in the Indian and Pacific oceans and feed on sea grasses, which has given rise to their common name, 'sea cows'. Manatees are found in the Atlantic and Caribbean, often living in coastal rivers and estuaries.

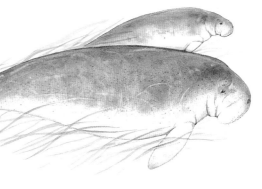

DID YOU KNOW?

The Weddell seal is one of the largest seals and holds the seal diving record. It can stay under for over an hour, and reach a depth of nearly 610 metres.

The polar bear eats fish, seals, and even walrus and beluga whales. It swims well, has partly webbed feet, a water-repellent coat, and a thick layer of fat.

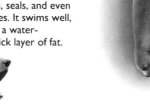

Baby harp seals have white coats for camouflage. Later they grow dark adult coats.

Marine iguanas

MARINE iguanas are equally good at clambering around the rocky shores of the Galapagos Islands and diving to depths of up to 15 metres. The only species of lizard living in the sea, they are very good swimmers with webbed feet and tails that are flattened sideways. They feed on seaweeds. Except for the breeding season, when the males often fight over the females, these otherwise harmless creatures spend their time in large groups, sometimes even lying one on top of another, warming themselves in the sun.

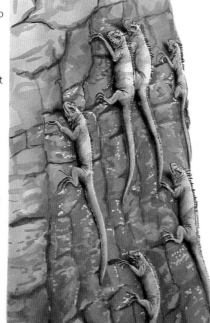

Baby turtles

Turtles have large flat legs and although bulky and ungainly on land, move gracefully in the water. They can reach speeds of up to 30 kilometres per hour. The female lays her eggs on shore, buried in the sand. At cooler temperatures more males are born; at hotter temperatures there are more females. When the young hatch, like these hawksbill turtles, they rush down the shore to the sea. Turtles in the Gulf of Mexico hibernate on the seabed during the winter.

Some of the largest whales, such as the blue, grey, and right whales, have no teeth. They feed by straining small animals and plankton through horny plates of baleen that hang like curtains from the roof of the mouth. A blue whale may eat up to two and a half tonnes of food every day.

The largest whale and the smallest dolphin

THE blue whale is the largest animal ever known, reaching over 30 metres in length – four times as big as any known dinosaur. It is found in all oceans but is now very rare. The Antarctic populations were only discovered this century but were quickly decimated. Over 29,000 blue whales were killed in one hunting season in the 1930s. The world population may now be down to a few thousand. Heaviside's dolphin (*below*) is probably the smallest cetacean, reaching just one and a half metres in length. It lives around South Africa in the Benguela current system, but little is known about it.

A whale breathes through a blowhole in the top of its head. The spout is formed by spray as the

whale blows out. Toothed whales have a single blowhole. Baleen whales have two blowholes and their spout has a forked appearance.

Whales, dolphins, and porpoises are a group of mammals called cetaceans. They have streamlined bodies and were once thought to be fish. The hindlimbs have been lost and the forelimbs have become fins or flippers. They swim by thrusting their tail flukes up and down in the water, unlike fish, which move their tails from side to side. Pilot whales can reach speeds of up to 48 kilometres per hour. Finback whales can dive to over 450 metres and swim for 40 minutes without breathing.

Breaching
Many whales and dolphins breach, or leap right out of the water. This may stun or panic fish shoals, and may also be a way of communicating with each other. The humpback whale (*left*), weighing more than 60 tonnes, manages to burst into the air and do a backward somersault! Some whales can also position themselves vertically with their head out of the water, a manoeuvre known as 'spy-hopping'.

Ending the hunt

WHALES have been hunted by humans since the time of the Vikings. The most important product was oil from the blubber, liver, and skeleton, that was used both for food and as a lubricant. The meat is also popular in some countries. The sperm whale produces a strange product in its intestine called *ambergris* that is used in the perfume industry. Traditionally, whales were hunted with harpoons from small boats and the carcasses were towed ashore. When factory whaling ships appeared in the 1920s, whales could be cut up and frozen on board and the harvest became more intensive. Gradually all the whales have been over-harvested.

The International Whaling Commission

This whale has been 'flensed', its skin completely stripped from its body.

Whales have no fur and keep warm with a layer of blubber under the skin, which is up to 50 centimetres thick in the bowhead whale. Most whales and dolphins have teeth and eat fish, squid, and other animals. They often hunt cooperatively, herding shoals of fish together by breaching and diving.

The sea unicorn

EARLY explorers called the narwhal the sea unicorn because of its single long tusk. This is formed by the spiral growth of the left tooth that can reach 3 metres in length. Usually, only the males have tusks. The function of the tusk is still not clear, although narwhals have been seen jousting.

Narwhals live in Arctic waters and feed on fish, shrimp, squid, and octopus.

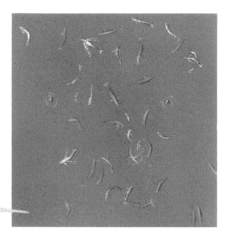

Beluga whales, white in colour, congregate in huge herds in North American estuaries during the breeding season (*above*). Belugas are known as the canaries of the sea because of their complex songs. Belugas also use facial expressions and often seem to be 'smiling'.

Common dolphin

The common dolphin is well known to us as one of the friendliest and most intelligent of marine animals. Normally living in groups, or 'schools', of up to a few hundred dolphins, they are among the fastest swimmers in the oceans, capable of reaching speeds of up to 40 km/h.

was set up in the 1940s to regulate harvests. Thanks to campaigns such as those by Greenpeace, most commercial whaling has now ceased. However, there is still some whaling by local people for food, and many of the smaller whales and dolphins are killed accidentally in big fishing nets on the high seas.

Killer whale

Found all over the world, including the polar seas, killer whales, or orcas, are closely related to dolphins. They are the only cetaceans to feed on mammals, such as seals and porpoises, as well as on seabirds, squid, and fish. They are able to take seal pups or penguins off the beach or ice (*below*).

Killer whales work together in groups of up to forty animals, called pods, when hunting. They circle the shoal of fish, herd of dolphins, or perhaps a rocky islet with basking seals, and once their prey is trapped, they strike. Their name is in recognition of their hunting prowess, but killer whales rarely attack humans.

BIRDS

Wandering albatross

The wandering albatross has the largest wingspan of any bird, up to three and a half metres in length. Gliders rather than fliers, they glide downwind from a height of about 15 metres and just before hitting the water turn into the wind that blows them back up again. They feed on fish, crustaceans, and squid which they seize from the surface.

Plunge diver

Many seabirds, including gannets, the brown pelican, boobies, and terns, are expert 'plunge divers'. By diving from great heights (in the case of gannets, up to 30 metres), they build up enough momentum to reach prey well below the surface. Despite the difficulty of this fishing method, terns are often successful in one dive out of three. Their skulls are strengthened to withstand the impact against the water.

Most pelicans can be found on inland bodies of water and do not dive. The brown pelican is mainly marine. When it catches sight of a fish it plunges vertically, straightening its neck just before entering the water. Having dived, it uses its expandable bill (common to all pelicans) to scoop up a large mouthful of fish.

Only about 300 species, or three per cent of the total number of different kinds of birds, live on the coast and oceans, but they make up for this by occurring in huge numbers. Enormous concentrations of seabirds are found in areas of upwelling (see page 8), such as in the Southern Ocean, and off the coasts of Peru and Chile. Some seabirds, like the albatrosses, spend almost their entire lives at sea, coming to land every other year to nest. Others, such as waders, ducks, and cormorants, are found along the shore all year round. Seabirds have a wide variety of feeding methods, from swimming underwater to catch fish, chasing other birds and forcing them to drop their prey, to plunge-diving into the sea themselves.

A guillemot bazaar

GUILLEMOTS breed on cliffs at closer densities than any other bird, often in bodily contact. There may be up to 70 pairs in one square metre, and their colonies are known as 'loomeries' or 'bazaars'. Despite this crowding, each pair defends a tiny territory. The eggs, as with many seabirds, are laid directly on the bare rock. Their colour and marking is very variable and helps the parents to recognize their own eggs. The chicks are recognized by their voices.

Eider duck

Most seabirds, and all sea ducks, have webbed feet for swimming. There are only a few true sea ducks, such as the eiders and scoters. The eider is found in large numbers in northern Europe. The female eider lines her nest with fine down feathers that she plucks from her breast. In Scandinavia the down is removed from the nests to make quilts or 'eiderdowns'.

Puffins

Seabirds breed in pairs, and many mate for life. Puffins lay a single egg at the ends of the burrows that they excavate with their beaks in turf on the cliffs. In larger colonies the ground can become honeycombed with burrows. The puffin's bill becomes brightly coloured to help it attract a mate.

A frigate bird display

FRIGATE birds are some of the best fliers, gliding on air currents and thermals (warm upcurrents) while seldom flapping their wings. The male has a red throat pouch that is inflated during courtship. The display is one of the best among seabirds. Males display on the nest site in groups of 30, spreading and vibrating their wings when females fly overhead, throwing back their heads and clacking their bills. When a female lands beside a chosen male, the pair snake their heads and necks across each other. The name, frigate bird, refers to its habit of obtaining food by harassing other birds in flight; a frigate is a warship.

DID YOU KNOW?

Rocky islets used by seabirds become covered with a thick layer of guano, or droppings. This is rich in phosphates, and in several areas, such as off the coast of Peru, it has been mined for fertilizer.

Gulls are the most familiar seabirds. They feed on fish and molluscs and can be seen dropping oysters or cockles from a height to break them on rocks below before eating.

The fairy (or white) tern lays a single egg precariously on a tree branch, without even building a nest. A single egg is easily concealed from potential predators.

Emperor penguins

Female emperor penguins lay a single egg which is then incubated by the male for 64 days on its feet. The female returns with food for the chick after it hatches.

Penguins are the best bird swimmers. They hunt for fish underwater, using their flipper-like wings.

Seabirds may return year after year to a safe site on cliffs and isolated islands to breed. They often form very large colonies in order to protect the eggs and young from predatory gulls, crows, and other invaders. Their black-and-white plumage helps to camouflage them when they are seeking fish. Many seabirds have been heavily hunted for their meat and eggs. Their eggs are vulnerable as they are often laid on the ground.

OCEAN MIGRATIONS

Pacific salmon

Pacific salmon spend most of their lives at sea. Small salmon, or smolts, feed on plankton at first, and then on fish. When they become adults, they travel to the American coast. They find the exact river in which they were born, using their excellent sense of smell. They battle upstream, leaping up waterfalls, to the shallow pools where they were born. Here they mate, and die shortly afterwards. The eggs hatch in spring, and for a few weeks the baby salmon feed on insects and crustaceans in the stream. Then they swim downriver to the sea and start the cycle again.

MANY animals make long journeys, either every year, or at different stages of their lives. Sometimes, as for the arctic tern, this is to take advantage of different sources of food. For others, such as the gray whale, it is to find a suitable place to breed. Some use the ocean currents and winds, like young eels that float back to Europe in the Gulf Stream. Many, incredibly, do it under their own power, including the spiny lobsters that tramp along the sea bottom. Various types of navigation systems are called into use. Birds use the sun's position to estimate compass directions. Salmon use smell to find the river where they were born. Scientists have found that if they block a salmon's nostrils it will get lost.

Migrating animals were a source of wonder to early naturalists. How eels reproduce was a mystery until the end of the last century because no one ever saw a baby eel. Aristotle thought they were formed from the soil. In the 18th century people thought that they came from the hairs of horses' tails and in the 19th century it was even suggested that a beetle gave birth to eels. The reason for the puzzle was that

Okhotsk Sea

ARCTIC OCEAN

Bering Sea

PACIFIC SALMON

NORTH AMERICA

GREY WHALE

SPINY LOBSTER

PACIFIC OCEAN

BAJA CALIFORNIA

Grey whale

The Californian grey whale migrates each spring and autumn along the west coast of North America. Its summer feeding grounds are in the shallow parts of the Bering Sea. The winter calving grounds are in the shallow lagoons of Baja California. When the calves are born, the whales return north. This is the longest migration of any mammal – a round trip of 20,500 kilometres every year. Its normal travelling speed on migration is 4.5 knots (8 km/h) although it can reach speeds of 11 knots (19 km/h). When migrating, it surfaces every three or four minutes and blows three to five times. The Korean grey whale makes a similar journey from the Okhotsk Sea off the coast of Siberia to the islands of South Korea. There used to be grey whales in the North Atlantic, but they have been hunted to extinction in this ocean.

RANGE OF EUROPEAN EEL

⬛	ONE YEAR
⬛	TWO YEARS
⬛	THREE YEARS
⬛	FOUR YEARS

Arctic tern

Arctic terns are the greatest travellers of all. They nest in the north, sometimes north of the Arctic Circle, in the northern summer. When only a few weeks old, the chicks set off on an 18,000-km journey south. They pass the western coasts of Europe and Africa, and travel across the Southern Ocean, to spend the southern summer on pack ice not far from the South Pole. By doing this, they take advantage of the very long summer daylight hours at both North and South poles for feeding. The arctic tern probably sees more daylight hours than any other animal.

adult eels live in fresh water, but migrate to the sea to breed. For many migratory land and shore birds, the oceans, offering them neither places to rest nor sources of food, are a major obstacle on their journey. They therefore tend to concentrate at points where the sea is narrowest in order to make the crossing. Many thousands of birds of prey, for example, cross the narrow Straits of Gibraltar in the spring and autumn on their way to and from Africa and northern Europe. Some birds follow routes that avoid large open stretches of water.

Spiny lobster

Spiny lobsters move south through the Caribbean in the autumn to spend winter in deeper waters. The migration happens at the onset of cold temperatures. As many as 100,000 individuals may migrate at a time, in single files of up to 60 animals. Each animal keeps in contact with the one ahead using its antennae to touch the other's abdomen. The white spots on their tails may help them keep in line. They may travel a total of 50 kilometres on the sea bottom.

EUROPE

AFRICA

EUROPEAN EEL

Sargasso Sea

ASCENSION ISLAND

ATLANTIC OCEAN

bean a

GREEN TURTLE

ARCTIC TERN

SOUTH AMERICA

Green turtle

The green turtle may travel thousands of kilometres to return to the same beach each year to lay her eggs. This is often the beach where she was born herself. Green turtles that feed off the coast of South America travel 4,800 kilometres every two to three years to breed on remote Ascension Island. Some green turtles make shorter coastal migrations, and a few, such as the Hawaiian population, stay in the same area all year round. Little is known about the male green turtles, but it is likely that they make similar migrations to the females.

European eel

European eels live in rivers but move down to the sea to breed. When about six years old, they travel some 6,400 kilometres across the Atlantic, taking between four and seven months to reach the Sargasso Sea. Here their eggs are laid in the deep, warm waters. After hatching, the young, transparent, leaf-shaped eels, called leptocephali or glass eels, drift back in the Gulf Stream, taking about three years to reach Europe. In the cooler, shallower waters they turn into young adults called elvers, and move up the rivers where they become fully grown adult eels, ready to start the cycle again.

THE OCEAN MARGINS

THE ocean margins include the coastline that we can see, as well as the continental shelf, continental slope, and continental rise that lie underwater *(see pages 16-17)*. The coastline varies from low, muddy, and sandy shores, to dramatic high rocky cliffs. Its form depends on the types of rocks and soils that make it up as well as the extent to which it is exposed to waves and winds.

The coastline is always changing, as some areas are eroded by waves and strong

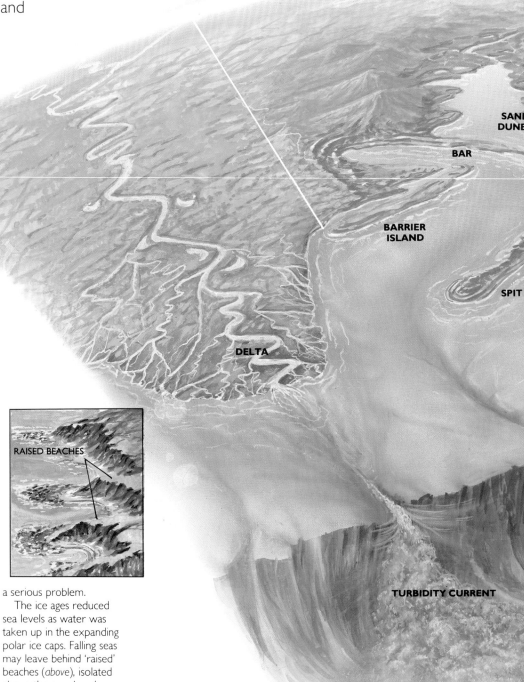

SAND DUNES

BAR

BARRIER ISLAND

SPIT

DELTA

TURBIDITY CURRENT

Sea levels

Sea levels are constantly changing and have a major effect on the appearance of coastlines. Since the end of the last Ice Age, sea levels have been rising slowly, but in the future they may rise much more rapidly. Human activities, such as the burning of fossil fuels, are increasing the amounts of carbon dioxide and certain other gases, known as greenhouse gases, in the atmosphere and these are causing the world to warm up. As this happens, glaciers will melt and release water into the sea, and the seawater will expand as its temperature increases. Any increase in sea level would be disastrous in places like Bangladesh *(left)* where much of the country is less than 4.5 metres above sea level and flooding is already

BANGLADESH

200–250 CM RISE

50 CM RISE

CURRENT SEA LEVEL

RAISED BEACHES

a serious problem.

The ice ages reduced sea levels as water was taken up in the expanding polar ice caps. Falling seas may leave behind 'raised' beaches *(above)*, isolated above the new beach which forms below it.

Coast formations

There are several types of coast formation. Deltas are formed at the mouths of large rivers that bring down enormous quantities of sediment. They extend up to 50 kilometres out to sea. The Mississippi is one of the largest deltas in the world, and the sediment is thought to be 10 kilometres thick.

Spits, bars, and barrier islands are formed when sand, gravel and shingle are deposited by the tide and waves. Dunes are formed by windblown sand.

At the mouths of estuaries large mud flats are formed in sheltered areas where there is little scouring action. Marshy coasts may develop in sheltered bays where sand and mud are deposited.

tidal currents while others grow and gradually creep seaward as mud, sand, and gravel are deposited. Large waves tend to erode the coast, but small waves stabilize beaches and deposit sediment. Waves usually strike the shore at an angle, so that sediments, having been eroded in one area, are carried along and deposited in another. Sometimes changes are very dramatic and sudden, as in a storm or hurricane, when large portions of coast may be washed away. Usually changes occur slowly over many years.

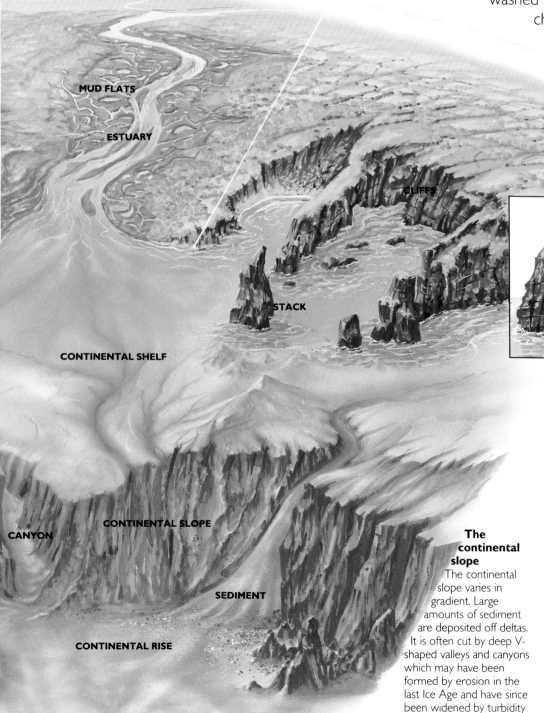

MUD FLATS

ESTUARY

CLIFFS

ARCH

STACK

CONTINENTAL SHELF

CONTINENTAL SLOPE

CANYON

SEDIMENT

CONTINENTAL RISE

Rocky coasts

Rocky coasts are usually the most scenic, particularly where erosion has caused complex chasms, pinnacles, caves, and arches (above). A hole in the roof of a cave may form a blowhole which makes strange noises as air and water are forced through it.

The continental slope

The continental slope varies in gradient. Large amounts of sediment are deposited off deltas. It is often cut by deep V-shaped valleys and canyons which may have been formed by erosion in the last Ice Age and have since been widened by turbidity currents. These are underwater avalanches that occur when large amounts of sediment resting on the upper continental slope are dislodged by earthquakes or their own weight. This mass of sediment, up to several kilometres in length and width and several hundreds of metres thick, rolls down the slope at speeds of up to 80 km/h.

The varied habitats found on the coast are home to a wide range of plants and animals. Coasts may be sheltered or exposed to wind and waves; they may be stony, sandy, muddy, or with cliffs. Coastal habitats also include coral lagoons, estuaries, and ice shelves. Where sand and mud is deposited in sheltered bays and estuaries, sea grasses, mangroves, and other marine plants can become established. These trap more silt and the marsh or mangrove swamp grows

A mangrove swamp

Unlike most trees, mangroves are able to tolerate salt, regular immersion in water, and the lack of oxygen in the muddy silt in which they grow. Their roots are specially adapted to obtain oxygen from the air. Some form buttresses or descend from branches as aerial roots while others protrude like little chimneys from the soil. Mangroves often have large floating seeds, that sometimes start to develop on the tree. The maze of roots traps sediment and provides a sheltered nursery for young fish and prawns. Mangroves are also a valuable source of fuelwood and timber. Despite their importance, mangroves are being destroyed worldwide and replaced with fish-farming ponds, houses, and marinas (see page 57).

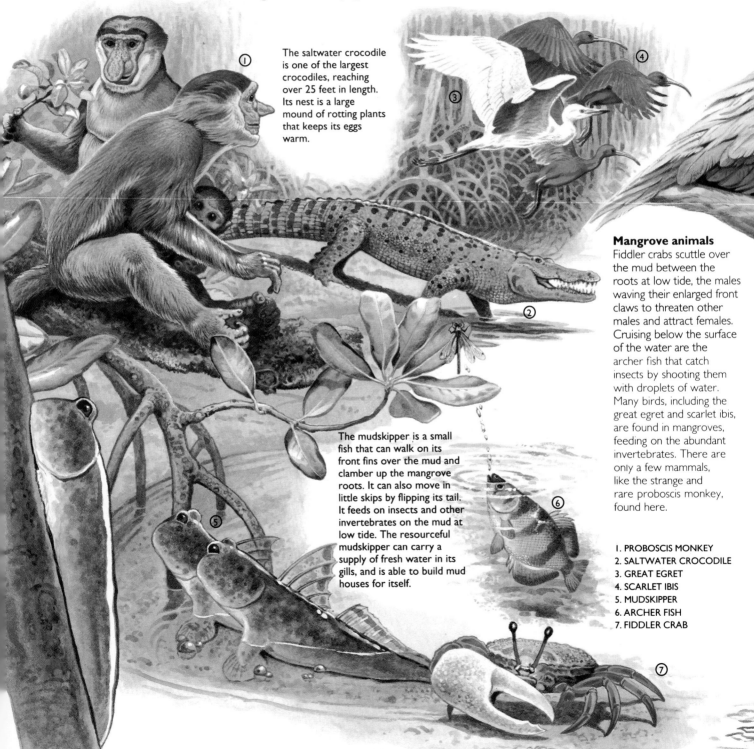

The saltwater crocodile is one of the largest crocodiles, reaching over 25 feet in length. Its nest is a large mound of rotting plants that keeps its eggs warm.

The mudskipper is a small fish that can walk on its front fins over the mud and clamber up the mangrove roots. It can also move in little skips by flipping its tail. It feeds on insects and other invertebrates on the mud at low tide. The resourceful mudskipper can carry a supply of fresh water in its gills, and is able to build mud houses for itself.

Mangrove animals

Fiddler crabs scuttle over the mud between the roots at low tide, the males waving their enlarged front claws to threaten other males and attract females. Cruising below the surface of the water are the archer fish that catch insects by shooting them with droplets of water. Many birds, including the great egret and scarlet ibis, are found in mangroves, feeding on the abundant invertebrates. There are only a few mammals, like the strange and rare proboscis monkey, found here.

1. PROBOSCIS MONKEY
2. SALTWATER CROCODILE
3. GREAT EGRET
4. SCARLET IBIS
5. MUDSKIPPER
6. ARCHER FISH
7. FIDDLER CRAB

Wading the waters

ESTUARIES, mud flats, and marshes are among the richest feeding grounds for many birds, and enormous flocks may congregate at low tides. These birds, often known as waders, have widely spaced toes that prevent them from sinking into the mud. Sandy and muddy shores often seem bare, with nothing on the surface at low tide, but hundreds of molluscs, ragworms, crustaceans, and sea urchins can be found by digging. Some waders, such as curlews, plovers, and sandpipers, are experts at this and their beaks are specially adapted. Others, like spoonbills, scoop up animals in the shallow waters.

out seaward. In tropical countries, mangroves are the main coastal vegetation. In cooler parts of the world, marshes are dominated by reeds, rushes, grasses, and other salt-tolerant plants.

The shore is 'zoned' with different plants and animals found at different levels, depending on how well they can cope with salinity and total immersion. This is seen particularly well on rocky shores where, as in northern Europe, each zone even has its characteristic type of periwinkle snail.

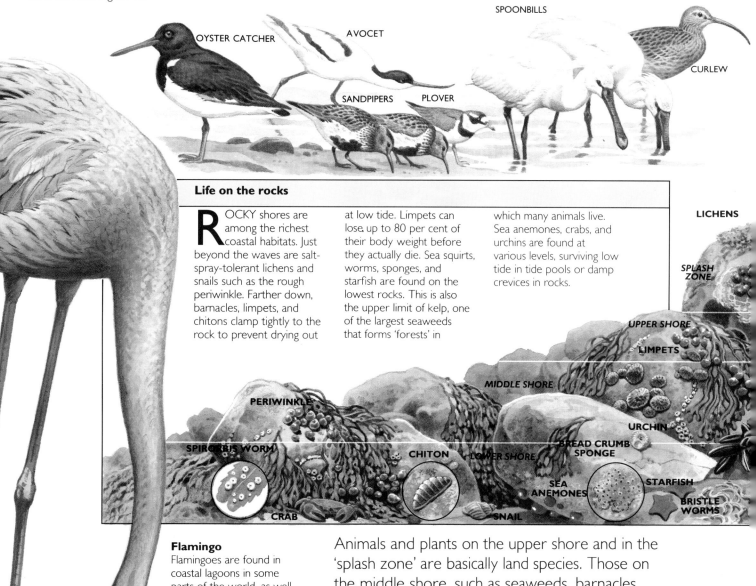

Life on the rocks

ROCKY shores are among the richest coastal habitats. Just beyond the waves are salt-spray-tolerant lichens and snails such as the rough periwinkle. Farther down, barnacles, limpets, and chitons clamp tightly to the rock to prevent drying out at low tide. Limpets can lose up to 80 per cent of their body weight before they actually die. Sea squirts, worms, sponges, and starfish are found on the lowest rocks. This is also the upper limit of kelp, one of the largest seaweeds that forms 'forests' in which many animals live. Sea anemones, crabs, and urchins are found at various levels, surviving low tide in tide pools or damp crevices in rocks.

Flamingo
Flamingoes are found in coastal lagoons in some parts of the world, as well as around inland lakes. The Caribbean flamingo (*left*), are the most brightly coloured. Their red or pink colour comes from pigments that occur in the food that they eat. They feed on algae and tiny animals by pumping water through their beaks.

Animals and plants on the upper shore and in the 'splash zone' are basically land species. Those on the middle shore, such as seaweeds, barnacles, and limpets, need a daily immersion in seawater. The lower shore is only uncovered at low spring tide: most animals here cannot survive out of water. In mangrove forests, different species are found as you move further inland, depending on the salinity, the amount of fresh water received from rivers, and the amount of tidal flooding.

CORAL REEFS

Types of reef

There are three main types of reef. Fringing reefs lie close to the shore along continental coasts and around islands. Barrier reefs lie at some distance from the shore. Atoll reefs, formed when a volcanic island 'sinks' and the reef continues to grow, are circular and often topped with small sandy islands.

ATOLL

VOLCANO

FRINGING REEF

1. EAGLE RAY	11. STARFISH
2. MORAY EEL	12. DAMSEL FISH
3. GIANT CLAM	13. THREAD-FIN BUTTERFLY FISH
4. SEA URCHINS	14. SPINY LOBSTER
5. SEA SLUG	15. BUTTERFLY FISHES
6. GROUPER	16. SURGEONFISH
7. CLEANER WRASSE	17. SOLDIERFISH
8. BRAIN CORAL	18. HAWKFISH
9. SEA ANEMONE	19. PARROT FISH
10. CLOWN FISH	20. FLASHLIGHT FISH

Polyps

The tiny coral animals called polyps secrete a stony, cup-shaped skeleton around them. The tentacles catch food although the coral gets most of its food from tiny single-celled plants that live inside the coral's tissues.

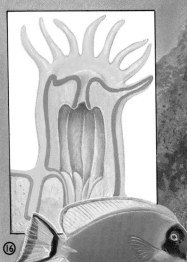

CORAL reefs are the richest, most colourful, and varied of all marine habitats. The greatest number of reef plants and animals are found in Southeast Asia where a single reef can contain 3,000 species. Reefs mainly grow in clear, shallow, tropical waters, extending slightly farther north or south where there are warm currents, as in Florida, Japan, and Australia. A reef is constructed of coral colonies that are very varied in shape and colour. Colonies are formed by tiny coral animals that divide to create new animals that lie on the skeletons of dead animals. Only the outside of a colony, therefore, has living animals on it. Brain corals grow slowly and have annual growth rings like trees. Some coral colonies have been found that are between 800 and 1,000 years old.

More species of fish can be seen on a reef than in any other habitat in the sea. They range from tiny gobies that live in crevices to large sharks that cruise along the edge of a reef looking for food. Butterfly fish are among the most colourful and are often seen in pairs. Clown fish live among the tentacles of sea anemones to protect themselves.

Spawning

Like other marine invertebrates, many corals reproduce by spawning. This means that the eggs and sperm are released into the water at the same time, where the sperm then fertilizes the egg. The baby coral that is formed is called a larva. On some reefs almost all the corals spawn on the same night of the year. On the Great Barrier Reef it happens in spring, in the week following full moon, just after dark.

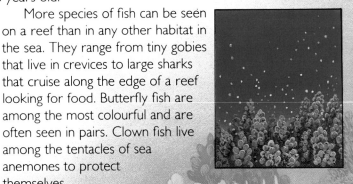

Molluscs are often difficult to see on a reef because they are well camouflaged and often nocturnal. Although awkward to spot, there are actually more species of mollusc than fish, with 4,000 species known from the Great Barrier Reef alone. Giant clams are an exception in that they are easily seen because of their brilliant blue mantles. On the reef there are also numerous crustaceans such as spiny lobsters and the banded cleaner shrimps that obtain food by picking parasites off fish. Sea urchins are also abundant and graze on small algae, breaking down dead coral in the process to form sand that eventually makes up the white coral sand beaches. Reefs are so crowded that many animals have had to develop ways to avoid being eaten or even sat on. One of the most effective methods is to become poisonous or develop dangerous spines, like the sea urchins. Reefs are often damaged by hurricanes and storms that break coral branches and topple whole colonies. But their greatest threat at present is from human activity. Ships and divers wreck fragile corals. Corals also die if sea temperature increases and there are fears that global warming might kill many coral reefs.

Coral jewels
The beautiful red and pink coral used to make jewellery does not come from coral reefs. It grows in deeper, cooler waters mainly in the Mediterranean where it is often found in caves and under overhangs, and also in the Pacific where large beds of it are found on seamounts.

Crown-of-thorns
The crown-of-thorns starfish (left) feeds on corals, sucking the living tissue up through its stomach and leaving the white coral skeletons. Outbreaks of these starfish have killed corals on many reefs, particularly in Australia.

A reef at night
A coral reef is quite different at night (below). Many corals expand their tentacles and some fish go to sleep among the corals, like the parrotfish that wraps itself in a protective mucous blanket that it secretes each night (bottom). The amazing flashlight fish is nocturnal and has a large gland under its eye that contains luminous bacteria that can be switched on and off.

EXPLORING THE OCEANS

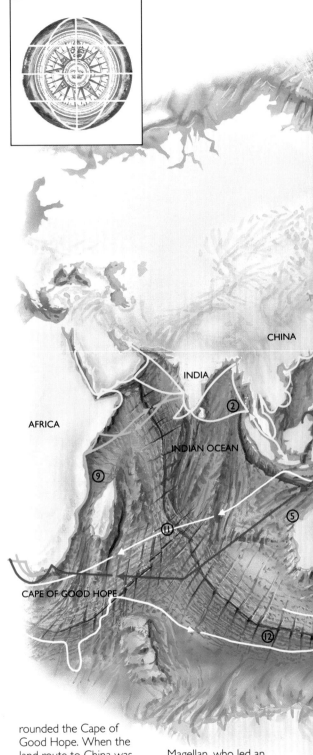

EARLY explorations of the oceans were largely driven by the need or desire to find new food and wealth, to achieve greater power, to spread religion — or out of simple curiosity. Another aim was to find better routes to places that were already known, although these voyages often resulted in the discovery of new lands. Many other peoples besides Europeans undertook such journeys. The Polynesians began colonizing the Pacific about 3,500 years ago. The Chinese explored the Asian seas in their junks and the Arabs, in their dhows, had charted much of the East African coast and reached India well before the Portuguese reached this area.

The Vikings

The Vikings explored the North Atlantic in the 9th and 10th centuries and reached North America. They set out from Scandinavia in their long ships, powered by about 60 rowers, to find new lands. Norse sagas say Iceland was so named because at that time it was so cold the fjords would freeze. In A.D. 982 the Viking Erik the Red found Greenland, at that time a much greener and more fertile land than Iceland.

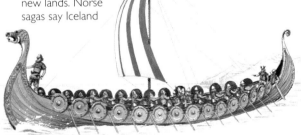

CHINA

INDIA

AFRICA

INDIAN OCEAN

CAPE OF GOOD HOPE

VOYAGES OF EXPLORATION

① VIKINGS 9TH-10TH CENTURIES
② ZHENG HE 1431-1433

IN THE SERVICE OF SPAIN

③ CHRISTOPHER COLUMBUS 1492-1493
④ AMERIGO VESPUCCI 1499-1500
⑤ MAGELLAN AND DEL CANO 1519-1522
⑥ ALVARO DE SAAVEDRA 1527-1528

IN THE SERVICE OF FRANCE

⑦ GIOVANNI DA VERRAZZANO 1524

IN THE SERVICE OF PORTUGAL

⑧ BARTOLOMEU DIAS 1487-1488
⑨ VASCO DA GAMA 1487-1498
⑩ AMERIGO VESPUCCI 1501-1502

JAMES COOK

⑪ FIRST VOYAGE 1768-1771
⑫ SECOND VOYAGE 1772-1775
⑬ THIRD VOYAGE (WITH CLERKE) 1776-1780

The Portuguese

The Portuguese were the great ocean explorers of the 15th century. They explored much of the west African coast, in search of gold and with the additional aim of converting Muslims to Christianity. Bartolomeu Dias sailed the full length of Africa in 1488 and rounded the Cape of Good Hope. When the land route to China was blocked by the Turks, the main aim was to find a sea route to the east. In 1497-98 Vasco da Gama sailed from Portugal to India, and opened the important spice trade routes with Southeast Asia. It was also a Portuguese, Ferdinand Magellan, who led an expedition (in the service of Spain) that completed the first circumnavigation of the world, a voyage that lasted from 1519 to 1522. He was killed in the Philippines and the expedition returned under Sebastian del Cano.

Scrimshaw
Right up until the last century, voyages on sailing and whaling ships could last for months or years, and in fine weather sailors had plenty of time for hobbies. Scrimshaw, the carving and engraving of whale teeth and bones and walrus tusks, was one of the most popular in the 19th century and developed into an art, particularly on the whaling vessels from the northeastern United States. The pictures are usually of ships and whaling, biblical or romantic scenes. The engravings were blackened with ink or any available dark pigment.

GREENLAND

ICELAND

SCANDINAVIA

①

GREAT BRITAIN

⑦

ATLANTIC OCEAN

PORTUGAL

SPAIN

③

BAHAMAS

④

⑤

AFRICA

⑧

HAWAII

⑥

⑤

APUA / GUINEA

PACIFIC OCEAN

⑤

⑪

⑨

⑫

TRALIA

⑫

⑪

⑪

⑪

NEW ZEALAND

⑩

⑫

⑫

STRAIT OF MAGELLAN

Columbus

In 1492 Christopher Columbus set sail from Spain, having failed to raise sponsorship from the Portuguese for his expedition.

In his flagship *Santa Maria*, with two other small ships and 120 men, he crossed the Atlantic hoping to find a quicker route to Asia and so give the Spaniards an advantage over the Portuguese who used the route around Africa. He landed in the Bahamas and continued on to Cuba, Haiti, and the Dominican Republic. On later journeys he discovered many other Caribbean islands as well as the coasts of Central and South America. After his death other explorers continued to explore the New World, including Amerigo Vespucci, for whom America is named.

Navigation

For ocean travel, navigation is a critical art. The Greeks developed a variety of instruments, including the astrolabe, which was used to map stars. The use of the magnetic compass became widespread in the 12th century. Used with charts, sailors could navigate out of sight of land. Latitude could be calculated by measuring the angle of the sun or stars above the horizon with a sextant. In 1735, the invention of the chronometer meant that accurate time could be kept on board ship, so that the distance from Greenwich, England, and thus the longitude, could be measured.

CHRONOMETER

COMPASS

ASTROLABE

SEXTANT

The early trans-oceanic voyages are among the most impressive because of the enormous difficulties and hardships that explorers and their crews had to face. Ships were cramped, uncomfortable, and unhygienic, and there was no way of keeping food fresh. Scurvy, a disease caused by lack of vitamin C, was a major problem. Vasco da Gama lost two-thirds of his crew on his voyage to India at the end of the 15th century. Scurvy could be prevented by eating fresh fruit, and Captain Cook lost no one on his second round-the-world journey in 1772, by insisting on an improved diet for his crew.

Kon-Tiki

To test the theory that the Polynesians originated in South America, crossing the Pacific in their canoes, Thor Heyerdahl tried the voyage in his balsa craft, Kon-Tiki. Although he successfully covered the 4,000 miles, anthropologists and historians have since proved that the Polynesians originated in Southeast Asia.

The Spirit of St. Louis

THE oceans were as much a challenge to early aeroplanes as they were to other methods of transport. The American Charles Lindbergh was the first person to fly alone nonstop across the Atlantic. A high-wing, single-engine monoplane was specially built for the

The voyages of Captain Cook

THE Englishman James Cook undertook three major voyages around the world between 1768 and 1779. He used the new navigational aids available in the 18th century to map the coasts of Papua New Guinea, New Zealand, and eastern Australia. He discovered many of the islands of the North and South Pacific, and crossed the Arctic and Antarctic circles. His final voyage was to find a northwest passage near Vancouver, but he failed. On his return, he stopped at Hawaii, which he had discovered on the outward journey. To the horror of his colleagues and crew, he was killed in a sudden quarrel with the local people.

Lone yachtsman
Joshua Slocum was the first person to sail single-handed around the world. He left Nova Scotia in his small wooden boat *Spray* in 1895 and returned to the same spot in 1898. He continued to sail alone until 1909, when he and his boat disappeared.

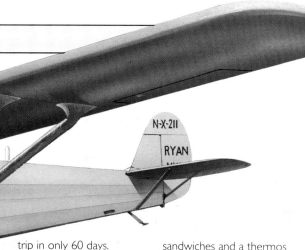

Another problem was that navigation instruments were extremely limited. Polynesian navigators could detect land by the colour of the sea, clouds, presence of birds, or simply the smell. In Europe, methods of calculating latitude (distance from the North Pole) were available by the 1480s but longitude (distance east or west) remained a problem until the 18th century.

Since routes across the oceans have been established, travellers have had to find other ways of achieving the same sense of adventure, by recreating early voyages, such as that of the Kon-Tiki, or lone yachting.

trip in only 60 days. Lindbergh helped to assemble each part of it himself. It was named the *Spirit of St. Louis* for the city that had financed the project. He chose a single engine as he wanted to minimize the number of potential mechanical problems. To cut down on weight he took no radio or parachute — only sandwiches and a thermos of coffee! In 1927 he successfully made the crossing from New York to Paris, in 33 hours 30 minutes, winning a prize of $25,000. Today, transatlantic flights take about seven hours, with Concorde, flying at supersonic speed, making the crossing in only three hours.

Zheng He
The 15th-century Chinese admiral Zheng He was one of the earliest ocean explorers. In his junk, he led voyages from China west to the Red Sea and East Africa, and south to Indonesia. The ocean-going junks of his time were larger than any ships built in the West at that time.

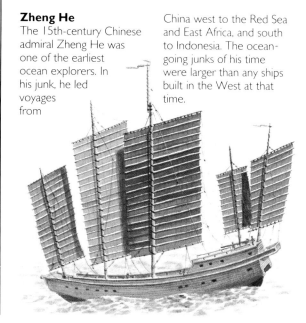

Egyptian papyrus boat
Some of the earliest ships were built in Egypt and were made of tapered reed bundles bound together like logs. This was because there were few trees in the region, only huge areas of swamp that provided papyrus. These boats were probably about 11 metres long.

Greek trireme
The classical Greek 'galleys', usually used as warships, were up to 30 metres long and 6 metres wide. The power of the galley was increased by having oarsmen at several levels. A bireme had two banks or decks of oars, a trireme (*left*) had three.
Triremes had as many as 170 oarsmen, with an additional crew of about 30, including a flautist!

Early Mediterranean ships relied on oars, but in northern Europe many ships had sails. These could only be used if the wind blew in the right direction. Careful positioning of the sails later meant that ships could sail against the wind. This made possible the great voyages of discovery of the 15th and 16th centuries.

Large sailing ships reached their full development in the clipper ships of the mid-1800s. By this time, however, the first ocean-going steamers, powered by screw propellers, were plying the seas.

Cruise liners
It is only in this century that ocean travel has become comfortable enough for people to go to sea purely for fun. Early travellers would join cargo vessels to see the world. The first cruise liners were built in the early 1900s and soon developed into huge luxury floating hotels.
The largest was the *Norway*: originally called the *France*, it was launched in 1961.

Floating castles

GALLEONS were the main sailing ships from 1500 to 1700. Looking much like floating castles, most had four masts and were square-rigged. Spanish galleons plied the trade routes of the Atlantic and Pacific in the 17th and 18th centuries.

Hydrofoils
The hydrofoil is one of the fastest modern boats. Stilts supported by underwater wings lift the hydrofoil's hull out of the water when it travels at speed. This cuts down on the 'drag' that slows up all vessels. Unfortunately, the hydrofoil's high fuel consumption makes it too expensive for long-distance travel, but it is used by ferry services throughout the world. The picture (*right*) shows a modern jet-propelled hydrofoil.

Computer ship
The *Shinaitoku Maru* was launched in 1980. Its two sets of rectangular sails are made of canvas stretched over steel frames. The ship also has a diesel engine. A computer monitors wind speed and direction and controls the sails, closing or opening them as required.

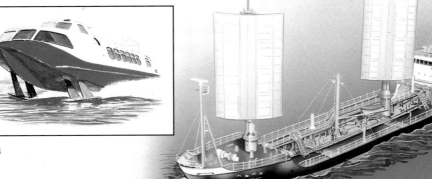

SHIPWRECKS

Truk Lagoon

Numerous wrecked ships lie scattered over the Pacific seabed as a legacy of the Second World War, but the most famous are those of Truk Lagoon in the Federated States of Micronesia. In 1944 U.S. bombers took by surprise a fleet of 60 Japanese merchant vessels and warships that had taken refuge in the lagoon. They sank every ship; over 1,000 men drowned. The fleet, scattered over the floor of the 65 kilometre-wide lagoon in about 75 metres of water, forms an enormous artificial reef and has become a popular diving site. Ships, such as the aircraft carrier *Fujikawa Maru* (below), are now encrusted with coral, algae, sponges, and other invertebrate life. Huge numbers of fish, including sharks, take shelter in the holds and cabins. The

EVEN for the best-built ships, the sea is a dangerous place. Storms are the main causes of losses, but many shipwrecks are the result of war at sea, bad navigation, or simple human error. For archaeologists and historians shipwrecks are literally buried treasure. They provide 'time capsules', showing how life was being lived at the time the ship went down. Preservation of wrecks has become a major science.

Even today there are still many accidents at sea, partly because the main shipping routes have become so crowded. For example, over 300,000 ships pass through the Straits of Dover each year.

wrecks have been designated a historical monument and no objects may be removed from them. Another famous casualty of the war was the German battleship *Bismarck*. It was sunk in the Atlantic in 1941 and now lies in more than 4,700 metres of water.

The *Titanic*

The *Titanic* was a British passenger liner, in her day the world's largest cruise ship. Many people thought her unsinkable. She was lost on her maiden voyage from Southampton to New York when she collided with a small iceberg just before midnight on April 14, 1912. The ship sank in just over two hours with the loss of about 1,500 lives. Seven hundred and eleven people were rescued. It

In 1982 a Turkish sponge diver discovered what proved to be the oldest-known shipwreck at Ulu Burun off the coast of Turkey. It dates from the 14th century B.C. and carried a huge range of valuable goods from all round the Mediterranean, including four-handled copper ingots.

TRUK ISLANDS

0   16 km

was not until a joint U.S.-French search project went to work in 1984-85, that the wreck was located.

EXPLOITING THE OCEANS

FOR centuries we have used the oceans as a source of food, minerals, and other valuable products, as a means of transport, and more recently for leisure activities. Seaweeds make good fertilizers, and are a source of substances used as thickeners in food. Salt has been extracted from seawater for over 4,000 years, and many minerals are mined offshore. The seabed is a source of sand and gravel for construction, and in some places huge quantities of dead shells are dredged and broken up to make cement.

Pearls
Pearls are produced by pearl oysters (below), when layers of nacre, or mother-of-pearl, are laid down around a speck of sediment or other foreign object inside the oyster's shell.

Krill

KRILL are the largest crustaceans in the rich plankton in the Southern Ocean. They feed on other plankton. 'Superswarms' of krill can be several kilometres wide and weigh up to two million tonnes. They are eaten by fish, penguins, other seabirds, and baleen whales. A single whale can get through four to five tonnes of krill in 24 hours. Since 1976, humans have been taking about 500,000 tonnes of krill a year, using them for food or fish meal. However, it is important that we do not overexploit krill as this could endanger whales and other animals that feed on krill.

ANTARCTICA

MAIN AREAS OF KRILL DISTRIBUTION

Offshore oil
Oil and gas form from the tiny plants and animals that lived in the sea millions of years ago. After they died and sank to the sea floor, they were covered in layers of sand and mud. The combination of pressure and a sealed environment turned them into droplets of oil trapped in tiny holes in the rock like water in a sponge.

In some places oil lies 2 kilometres below the present seabed. Oil rigs (right) have a drill which bores into the rock; the oil or gas is then pumped up and taken to land by pipelines or tankers. Offshore oil provides about one quarter of the world's total, or about 15 million barrels a day.

Manganese nodules

Manganese nodules are strange lumps found on the seabed. They form when elements in seawater are deposited around fragments of material such as fish bones and shark teeth. They contain high concentrations of nickel, cobalt, and copper, all of which are useful to humans. The best nodules are found where there is little sediment and stable conditions, as in the large deep ocean basins. There are an estimated 1,500 trillion tonnes of nodules in the Pacific.

Tidal power

The sea generates energy through waves and tides that can be converted into a form we can use. The world's first commercially operated tidal power barrage is on the River Rance in Brittany, France (below). As the tide rises and passes through tunnels in the dam, water drives propellers of an engine in the tunnels, producing electricity.

Fishing

Today, fish provide about 15 percent of all animal protein consumed. Fish products are used for animal feed, fertilizers, and soaps. Some modern fishing vessels have equipment that can take an entire shoal from the sea in one haul. Care has to be taken that catches do not exceed the rate at which a stock replenishes itself.

Tourism

The sea and its shores are the most popular holiday destinations. Sandy beaches, cliffs, and scenic coastlines draw millions of visitors and there are many leisure activities to be enjoyed in or on the ocean, such as surfing, sailing, scuba diving, snorkelling (above), and fishing. Even the high seas are now used by the tourist industry, with big cruise ships sailing across the oceans to visit remote islands.

It is possible to increase the abundance of fish in some places. One method is to build artificial reefs. These act like coral reefs, providing shelter for fish and invertebrates. Once they become covered with seaweed, corals, and other animals they provide a perfect fish habitat. They are best if made of concrete or bamboo, but tyres and even old cars are sometimes used.

Fishing the traditional way

EARLY humans used very simple methods for fishing, and these are still used in many countries. The simplest are harpoons and hooks-and-lines. Fishermen use small boats such as dug-out canoes and usually stay close to shore. The invention of nets meant that large numbers of fish could be caught at once. To find shoals, traditional fishermen watch seabirds and look for ripples on the surface of the sea. Fish can also be caught in traps, while molluscs, crabs, and small fish are collected by hand or by digging when walking over coral reefs, rocks, or muddy shores at

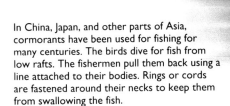

In China, Japan, and other parts of Asia, cormorants have been used for fishing for many centuries. The birds dive for fish from low rafts. The fishermen pull them back using a line attached to their bodies. Rings or cords are fastened around their necks to keep them from swallowing the fish.

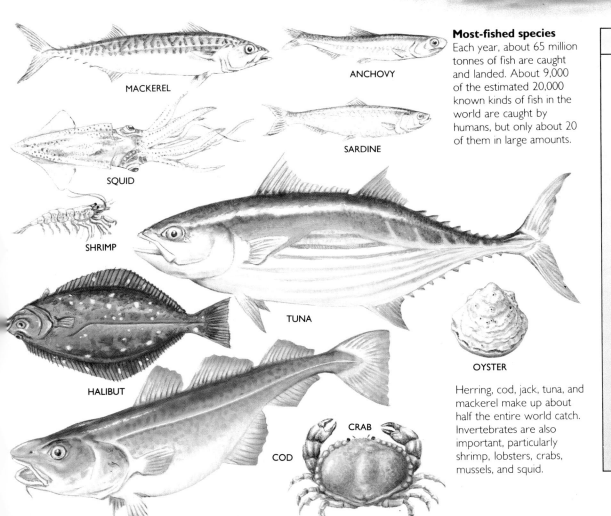

MACKEREL

ANCHOVY

SQUID

SARDINE

SHRIMP

TUNA

HALIBUT

OYSTER

COD

CRAB

Most-fished species
Each year, about 65 million tonnes of fish are caught and landed. About 9,000 of the estimated 20,000 known kinds of fish in the world are caught by humans, but only about 20 of them in large amounts.

Herring, cod, jack, tuna, and mackerel make up about half the entire world catch. Invertebrates are also important, particularly shrimp, lobsters, crabs, mussels, and squid.

Taking the catch

COMMERCIAL fishing fleets go to sea in large ships and may be away several months. They often have a factory ship that processes or refrigerates the fish. Sonar equipment and even space satellites may be used for locating schools of fish. Shoaling species such as anchovies are taken in purse seines. Tuna in the open seas are fished with drift nets stretched for

DRIFT OR GILL NET

low tide.

Some fishermen have very specialized methods. In Mauritania, fishermen throw out their nets when dolphins swim close to shore intending to round up shoals of fish on which to feed themselves. In Sri Lanka, some fishermen sit on tall stilts to have a good view of fish below, without the fish seeing them.

Fish preservation

Fish must be preserved if they are to be kept for any length of time. The simplest method is to dry them in the sun on racks. Other ways include smoking or soaking in very salty water called brine. The most common methods of preservation used today are refrigeration and canning.

Humans have gathered food from the sea since prehistoric times. In Japan and Iceland, fish is eaten in much greater quantities than meat, and some Pacific islanders rely almost entirely on fish for protein. Over one quarter of the world catch is converted into fish oil, animal feed, and fertilizers or used in products such as soaps and drugs. The world fishery catch is over 98 million tonnes a year, a big increase since the 1950s when only about 20 million tonnes were taken annually. In addition, about 24 million tonnes a year are taken by local fishermen and eaten in their own villages. The increase is because of the growing human population and the development of more efficient methods of catching fish. Unfortunately, it has led to overexploitation of more than 90 per cent of commercial fisheries.

World fishing grounds

The biggest commercial fisheries are in the northern Pacific and northern Atlantic. In 1991 the world's top fishing nations were Japan, USSR and China. Countries now have the rights to fishing within 320 kilometres of their coasts. The richest fishing grounds are the continental shelves and areas of upwelling, where cold water rich in plankton and food rises to the surface. Vast quantities of anchovy used to be caught off Peru but the catch dropped dramatically after a succession of damaging El Niños (see page 9).

hundreds of kilometres. Bottom trawls and seine nets are used to catch fish that live on the seabed and generally take several different kinds at once. Shallow-water coastal fish are driven into traps, or caught there by currents and tidal flows. Squid are fished in the Antarctic with 'jiggers', hooks on lines that are bounced up and down.

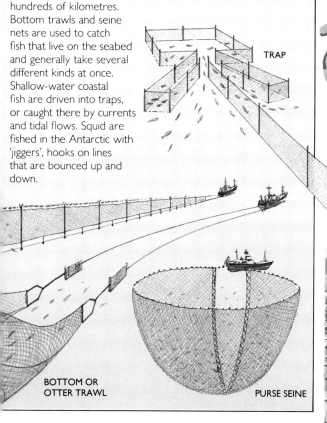

TRAP

BOTTOM OR OTTER TRAWL

PURSE SEINE

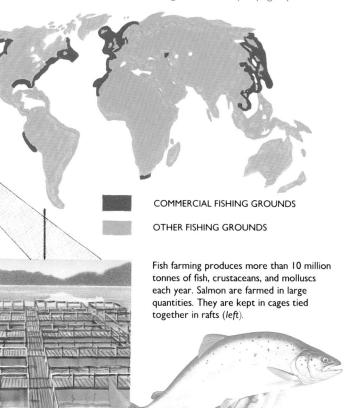

COMMERCIAL FISHING GROUNDS

OTHER FISHING GROUNDS

Fish farming produces more than 10 million tonnes of fish, crustaceans, and molluscs each year. Salmon are farmed in large quantities. They are kept in cages tied together in rafts (left).

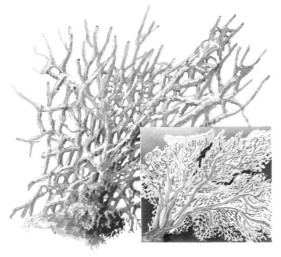

Killing coral

Coral reefs are damaged by tourists and ships. Corals also 'bleach' (turn white) and may die if stressed by increased sea temperatures or some pollutants. They are also easily suffocated by silt, washed off the coast or down rivers as a result of deforestation, or stirred up from the sea bottom during dredging.

Polluting the oceans

SOME pollution in the oceans comes from ships or offshore operations, but a large proportion results from human activities on land. Oil, sewage, and garbage are some of the pollutants we dispose of in the sea. Over two million tonnes of oil are discharged into the oceans each year, a quarter from ships and the rest from on-shore operations.

Plankton blooms, or red tides, are sudden vast population explosions of plankton caused by increased nutrients in the water, usually from sewage or agricultural runoff containing fertilizers. Large quantities of waste uses up oxygen in the water in the process of rotting. Eventually, even the seabed can be starved of oxygen, as in the Baltic Sea where nearly half of the deep waters are now virtually devoid of life.

Garbage in the oceans has increased dramatically since the invention of plastics and other synthetic materials that are buoyant and do not disintegrate (some can survive for as long as 50 years). Plastic containers, packaging, and a wide variety of toys float to remote areas on the ocean currents. Turtles and whales die from eating floating plastic that looks like jellyfish.

POLLUTION

SEVERE

PERSISTENT

MEDITERRANEAN SEA

OIL SPILL

PLANKTON BLOOM

Mediterranean pollution

The Mediterranean is bordered by 18 countries, with at least 120 major cities that pour sewage and industrial wastes into the sea. As it is almost landlocked, pollutants are not washed away as in the open sea, and they tend to become more concentrated over time. Hundreds of striped dolphins died in the Mediterranean in 1990. A virus was found in some of them similar to one found in seals that died in the North Sea over the same period. These diseases may be linked to pollution, although this has not yet been confirmed.

In 1975, Mediterranean countries jointly set up an Action Plan to fight pollution. There has been no increase in pollution since then, but there are still many problems to be solved.

Oiled seabirds

SEABIRDS are very vulnerable to oil spills as oil destroys the waterproofing of their feathers and they become waterlogged. While trying to clean themselves, they eat the oil which then poisons them. Up to 30,000 birds are thought to have died as a result of oil spills during the 1991 Gulf War. The *Exxon Valdez*, a supertanker that went aground in 1989 in Prince William Sound, Alaska, spilled 11 million gallons of oil, killing over 36,000 seabirds and 1,000 sea otters, and affecting over 1,600 kilometres of coastline.

ABOUT 150,000 tonnes of plastic nets and lines are discarded by fishermen each year, over 800 kilometres of plastic fishing nets in the North Pacific alone. These entangle turtles, seabirds, and many marine mammals. Today, much fishing is carried out with fine plastic drift nets that are so large and sheer they cannot be seen by diving birds or detected by dolphins with their sonar. Commercial fishing fleets may set up to 32,000 kilometres of net a day in the fishing season with a single net stretching for up to 50 kilometres. They are used in all oceans for catching tuna, squid, salmon, and other fish. In the Pacific about 100,000 dolphins and millions of birds have been killed by becoming entangled in these nets. Other modern fishing methods also kill animals accidentally in large numbers; for example shrimp trawls that catch turtles.

Since about three quarters of the world's population lives on the coast, it is not surprising that the oceans are suffering from pollution and other human activities. Unfortunately, people have always thought of the oceans as rubbish dumps. Even people living inland are not blameless; rivers carry 9.3 thousand million tonnes of silt and waste to coastal waters each year. Coastal habitats, such as marshes, are threatened by the building of ports, factories, tourist resorts, and other developments and these are the areas where marine plant and animal life is richest.

GARBAGE

Dinoflagellates are the tiny plankton that suddenly bloom and cause red tides when the level of nutrients rises in seawater. Species called *Gonyaulax* and *Glymnodium* can be highly poisonous and can contaminate seafood that we eat.

Dynamite fishing
In some countries, fishermen use methods that cause serious damage to the seabed. In the Philippines, dynamite explosions stun the fish that then float to the surface where they can be collected in a net. But these explosions also kill the coral reef and many other plants and animals.

Mangrove destruction
Mangroves are being cut down worldwide for timber, fuelwood and wood chips. In the Philippines, the total area of mangroves declined from 33,000 to only 2,600 square kilometres between 1920 and 1988. In many countries, such as Ecuador and Indonesia, mangroves are destroyed to make ponds for rearing prawns and fish.

The main forms of pollution are sewage and industrial waste. Chemicals, pesticides, and other industrial products are common pollutants and have been found in penguins, arctic seals, and even in rat-tail fish at a depth of 3,000 metres. Beluga whales in the St Lawrence River in North America, whose population has dropped from 5,000 to 460, have themselves become toxic; they contain the highest levels of poisons found in any marine mammal.

In some countries, particularly in the Pacific, costal villagers traditionally 'own' nearby areas of sea and coral reef and have the right to fish there. They are usually careful not to take too many fish and not to use damaging fishing methods. Sometimes they stop fishing for part of the year or in a particular place to allow fish stocks to recover.

Conserving the reefs
All round the world efforts are being made to prevent further damage to coral reefs. In Indonesia, a large marine park is being set up to protect the reefs and threatened animals (1). The marine parks at Eilat, in the Red Sea (2), and Buck Island, in the U.S. Virgin Islands (3), have underwater nature trails for divers. Mooring buoys on reefs in Hawaii (4), American Samoa (5), Florida (6), and other places in the Caribbean stop boats from anchoring on fragile corals.

Some overexploited reef animals are 'farmed' or raised in tanks, such as the queen conch in the Turks and Caicos islands in the Caribbean (7), giant clams in the Solomon Islands (8), and trochus snails, that provide the valuable mother-of-pearl shell, in Palau in the Pacific (9).

At 345,000 square kilometres the Great Barrier Reef Marine Park off Australia is the largest coral reef reserve in the world (*right* and 10 on map). It is divided into zones for research scientists, tourists, and fishermen.

REEFS

CAIRNS

CORAL SEA

TOWNSVILLE

0   160 km

CORAL REEFS

LOGGERHEAD TURTLE

BLUE WHALE

SEA OTTER

New mangrove forests
Attempts are now being made to restore mangrove forests that have been very badly damaged. In several countries, such as India, Bangladesh, and Ecuador, small seedlings are planted out in the mud in areas where the forests have been destroyed.

These traditional forms of conservation have broken down in many areas, but people are now realizing how important it is to maintain them wherever possible.

Pollution, and overfishing in the open oceans outside countries' exclusive fishing zones, are more difficult problems to deal with. Often nations have to work together to find solutions. Many countries have drawn up treaties and

Protected species?
Most threatened marine species are now legally protected, although unfortunately this does not always mean that they are not killed. Many seals and whales are protected, but there is still much concern over the future of some whales as countries such as Norway and Japan still wish to continue whaling.

The best hope for the future of the giant clam lies in the farming projects being started in many countries. Sea otter populations have recovered dramatically since this species has been protected. Turtles are protected in most countries and trade in their shells, skins, and meat is banned.

Whale-watching

THE tourist industry can play an important role in protecting the marine environment, on which it depends in so many countries. Whale-watching trips *(below)* are a way of making an income from whales without killing them. Hotels, scuba diving businesses, and other tourist operators are now helping to protect coral reefs. Some hotels set up reserves to educate tourists about the fragility of coral reefs. Clean beaches are essential to the tourist industry, and in Europe official standards have now been set to limit sewage pollution.

MONK SEAL

GIANT CLAM

Saving the turtles

Many turtle populations are declining because the eggs are eaten by humans or other predators, or nesting females are disturbed by tourists. In Pakistan, and many other countries, nesting beaches are now patrolled at night. Guards remove eggs to artificial nests in protected enclosures. When the baby turtles hatch, they are released into the sea. These projects help local people to understand why turtle eggs should not be taken and can also provide a tourist attraction.

regional conventions with each other in which they agree to work together to stop pollution and overfishing.

Marine parks and reserves have been set up in numerous countries to protect threatened marine species and vulnerable habitats such as mangroves, coral reefs, swamps, and estuaries.

We can all play a part in helping to protect the oceans. We can visit marine parks and reserves, learn about marine life, and support conservation organizations that are working to save the seas. We can recycle plastic, glass, and paper to cut down on waste, and avoid buying products that use a lot of energy. When visiting the coast and sea, we can make sure that we do not pollute it or damage its precious marine life.

Rainbow Warrior

MANY conservation organizations have helped save threatened marine animals and their ocean habitats. The World Wide Fund for Nature (WWF) has helped to set up marine parks in many countries and has supported projects to protect turtles, whales, and seals. The Ocean Voice International works in the Philippines (11 on map), training Philippine fishermen to catch aquarium fish with nets instead of using poison, which damages coral reefs.

Greenpeace has paid particular attention to the survival of the oceans. Its best known ship, *Rainbow Warrior*, was named after a legendary Red Indian tribe called the "Warriors of the Rainbow" who, it was said, would restore the Earth to its former beauty. Greenpeace has mounted campaigns against testing nuclear weapons in the Pacific, against whaling and sealing, and against the dumping of chemical and radioactive wastes in the oceans. Greenpeace members often take dramatic action to achieve their aims, for example, placing themselves in the paths of large whaling boats. They have also persuaded people to stop buying brands of canned tuna that have been taken with drift nets, which kill dolphins.

GLOSSARY

Abyssal plain   Extensive flat area of the ocean floor formed by sediment, washed off the continents, lying over the ocean crust.

Asthenosphere   The hot, molten inner layer of the Earth.

Astrolabe   An instrument used to map the stars.

Atoll   A coral island made up of a reef surrounding a lagoon.

Baleen   Horny plates that hang from the jaws of toothless whales and are used for straining plankton from the water.

Beaufort Scale   A system used to describe the strength of the wind at sea, using signs that can be seen by the naked eye.

Benthic   Animals and plants that live on or in the ocean floor.

Blubber   A thick layer of insulating fat under the skin of cetaceans and seals.

Breach   The way in which whales and dolphins leap out of the water.

Cetacean   The group of animals comprising whales, dolphins, and porpoises.

Clipper   A large, fast sailing ship that carried cargo across the major oceans in the last century.

Continental rise   The rise often found at the base of the continental slope formed by the sediment that rolls down.

Continental shelf   The part of a continent that extends out below the surface of the sea.

Continental slope   The steep slope that drops off from the edge of the continental shelf to the ocean floor.

Convergence   Place in the ocean where currents meet, usually causing water to sink.

Coral reef   A stony structure formed from living corals and numerous other invertebrates, plants, and fish, found in tropical seas.

Crustaceans   Invertebrate group characterized by hard outer skeletons and jointed legs.

Cyclone   Violent storm (also called hurricane or typhoon) that occurs when warm, moist air rises over tropical oceans.

Delta   The muddy or sandy mouth of a large river, broken into numerous channels, and formed by sediment brought down by the river.

Denticles   Tiny tooth-like projections that cover the skin of sharks and some other animals.

Divergence   Place in the sea where currents part, usually causing water to rise.

Gill   Feather-like organ found in many marine invertebrates and fish that is used for respiration.

Hot spot   Place where hot magma rises to the surface of the ocean bed and forms chains of volcanoes, as the plates move over it.

Invertebrate   Large group of animals, including insects, molluscs, and crustaceans, that have no backbone or internal skeleton.

Latitude   Distance north and south of the equator.

Lithosphere   The rigid outer surface of the Earth.

Longitude   Distance east or west of Greenwich, England.

Mangrove   Tree that grows on muddy coasts in tropical countries whose roots are adapted to regular flooding by high tides, salty water, and lack of oxygen.

60

Migration	The movement of an animal from one part of the world to another on a regular basis (for example, annually or seasonally to find food or breeding areas).
Molluscs	A large group of invertebrates that includes snails, slugs, bivalves, octopuses, squids, and many others, many of which have protective shells.
Monsoon	A season characterized by different patterns of winds and rainfall that occurs in some parts of the tropics.
Navigation	The skill of getting vehicles or vessels from one place to another.
Neap tide	Tide that occurs when the Sun and Moon are at right angles to the Earth, giving the smallest tidal range.
Ocean ridge	A long range that rises above the seafloor as a result of new seafloor welling up from inside the Earth.
Ocean trench	A long, narrow, very deep valley found near the edge of continents or island chains, also called subduction zone as this is where one plate moves under another.
Pack ice	The layer of ice floating on the sea, formed when the sea freezes, which constantly breaks up and becomes 'packed' together again.
Pelagic	Living or growing at or near the surface of the ocean, as certain animals or plants.
Plankton	The tiny plants (phytoplankton) and animals (zooplankton) that float in the surface layers of the oceans and provide food for numerous marine animals.
Scrimshaw	Whale teeth, bones, and walrus tusks carved or engraved with pictures.
Sextant	Instrument used to measure the angle of the Sun and stars above the horizon.
Sonar	A device used for locating and measuring the distance of other objects underwater.
Spring tide	Tide that occurs when the Sun and Moon are in line with the Earth, giving the largest tidal range.
Stromatolites	Hard, cushion-like structures, formed by blue-greens, that are the earliest forms of life in the sea.
Submersible	An underwater vessel, much smaller and more manoeuvrable than a submarine that usually has some kind of motor and can carry passengers.
Swim bladder	The air sac found in bony fish that prevents them from sinking.
Thermal vent	A 'chimney' found in some parts of the deepest oceans where sulphur-rich hot water from below the Earth's crust is released.
Thermocline	An abrupt temperature change in tropical oceans at about 300 metres where deep cold waters meet warm surface waters.
Tidal range	The difference in height between high and low tides.
Turbidity current	An underwater avalanche that flows down the continental slope, carrying huge quantities of sediment.
Upwelling	Cold waters that rise up from the deep into warmer surface waters, often found at divergences.
Waterspout	A whirling mass of air that forms over warm water when rising, warm, moist air meets cold, dry air.
Whirlpool	A circular movement of water caused when two currents meet or when strong tides and currents meet.

INDEX

A

abyssal plains 17, 26, 60
albatrossess 22, 23, 36
Alvin 17, 20-21
ambergris 34
ammonites 25
amphipods 27
angel fish 31
angler fish 23, 27, 31
Antarctic Ocean 6, 12, 22
archer fish 42
Arctic Ocean 6, 12, 23
Argo 14
artificial reef 44, 54
asthenosphere 18, 60
astrolabe 48, 60
Atlantic Ocean 6, 8-9, 10, 16, 18, 19
Atlantis 14
atolls 19, 23, 60
auks 23
avocets 43

B

baleen 34, 60
Baltic Sea 6
barnacles 9, 29, 43
barrier islands 40-41
bars 40-41
bathyscapes 21
bathyspheres 21
Bay of Fundy 13
bays 12
Beaufort Scale 11, 60
Beaver IV 21
benthic 22, 60
Bering Sea 6, 38
Bermuda Triangle 15
bladder wrack 22
blubber 32, 34, 60
blue-greens (cyanobacteria) 24
boobies 36
breach 34, 60
brittle stars 26
Burgess shale fossils 25
butterfly fish 22, 44

C

Caribbean Sea 6, 10, 12
cetaceans 34, 60
Challenger 20
Challenger Deep 21
chitons 43
Christmas tree worm 28
chronometer 48
clams 17, 23, 44, 58-59
cleaner wrasse 44
clipper ships 10, 60
clown fish 44
coastlines 18, 40-41
coasts 13, 42-43
cockles 26
cod 26
coelacanths 24-5
compass 48
computer ship 50
cone shells 28
continental movements 18
continental rise 16, 40, 60
continental shelf 16, 40, 60
continental slope 16-17, 40-41, 60
convergences 9, 60
copepods 27
coral 22, 23, 26, 28, 44-45
coral reefs 6, 19, 60
    conservation 58-59
    damage to 56-57
    life on 23
cormorants 36, 54
crabs 42
    giant spider 22, 23
    horseshoe 25
crinoids (feather stars) 28-29
crocodiles 42
cruise liners 50
crustaceans 23, 29, 60
curlews 43
currents 8-9, 19, 41
cuttlefish 26
cyclones 10, 11, 60

D

Deep Diver 21
deltas 41, 60
denticles 30, 60
dinoflagellates 27, 57
diurnal tide cycles 12
divergences 8, 9, 60
diving saucer 21
diving suits 20-21
Doldrums 10
dolphins 34
DSRV 21
dugongs 15, 33
dunes 41

E

eagle rays 14
eels 38-9
    conger 26
    European 39
    gulper 26
    moray 44-45
eider ducks 37
egrets 42
Egyptian papyrus boats 50
El Niño 9, 55
estuaries 12, 43
explorers 46-47, 48-49
Exxon Valdez 7, 56

F

feather stars (crinoids) 28-29
fishing 53, 54-55, 57
fishing grounds (world) 55
fish preservation 55
flamingoes 43
flashlight fish 44
flatfish 31
flounders 31
FNRS-3 21
food cycle (of the oceans) 26
fossils 24-25

G

Galapagos 9, 33
galleons 50
galleys 50
gannets 26, 36
giant squid 15, 28
giant vase sponge 28
gills 30, 60
glaciers 7, 12
Great Barrier Reef 44-45
    Marine Park 58-59
Greek trireme 50
Greenpeace 35, 59
grouper fish 44
guillemots 36
Gulf Stream 8
gulls 37

H

halibut 31
hatchet fish 26
hawkfish 44
helmet shells 22
herring 27
Hesperornis 24
hot spots 19, 60
hurricanes 10, 41
hydrofoils 50

I

ibises 42
icebergs 7, 12-13
ichthyosaurs 24
Indian Ocean 6, 8, 16, 17, 19, 22
International Whaling
    Commission 34
invertebrates 28, 60
islands 19
isopods 27

J

Jason 21
Jason and the Argonauts 14
jellyfish 24, 28, 29

Jim 20
junks 49

K

kelp 22, 26, 42-43
kraken monster 15
krill 22, 27, 52

L

latitude (see navigation) 60
limpets 17, 43
lingula 27
lithosphere 18, 60
longitude (see navigation) 60
lumpsucker 26-27

M

maelstrom (whirlpool) 12
manatee 23
manganese nodules 53
mangroves 26, 42, 43, 57,
    58-59, 60
Marie Celeste 14
marine iguanas 9, 23, 33
marine plants 22
marine worms 28
marshy coasts 40-41, 43
Mediterranean Sea 6, 12, 15,
    19, 29, 56
mermaids 15
Mid-Atlantic Ridge 7
migration 38-39, 61
Mississippi delta 41
Moby Dick 15
molluscs 23, 26, 27, 29, 31, 61
monsoon 8, 11, 61
mud flats 41, 43
mudskippers 26, 42

N

narwhals 23, 35
Nautilus 20

nautilus 25
navigation 61
    in animals 38
        instruments 48-49
navigators 7, 48-49
neap tides 12, 61
Neptune 14
nets 54-55, 56-57
nutrients 26

O

oar fish 27
oceans 19, 26
    currents 8-9
    facts about 6, 8 ,11, 13
    floors 7, 16, 17, 18
    how formed 24-25
    ridges 6-7, 18, 61
    trenches 6-7, 18, 61
octopuses 15, 23, 26, 29
oil 7, 20, 27, 52, 56-57
Opisthoproctus soleatus 27
oyster catchers 43

P

Pacific Ocean 6-7, 8, 16-17, 18,
    23, 56-57
pack ice 12-13, 23, 61
parrot fish 22, 44
pearls 52
pelagic 22, 61
pelicans 23, 36
pen shells 29
penguins 22, 23, 37
periwinkles 26, 43
Perry 21
Persian Gulf 13
Photichthys argenteus 27
phytoplankton 22, 27
pillow lava 19
pirates 15
Pisces 21
plaice 26, 31
plankton 22, 26, 28, 56-57, 61
plate tectonics 16-17, 18-19
plesiosaurs 24
plovers 43
polar bears 22, 33
polar oceans 12, 13

pollution (of the oceans) 56-57
polyps 44
porpoises 30, 34
Portuguese man-of-war 28
prawns 22
proboscis monkey 42
pufferfish 31
puffins 37

R

raised beaches 40
rat-tail fish 26
rays 30
Red Sea 12, 19, 22
rocky coasts 40
ROVs 21

S

salmon 38, 55
San Andreas Fault 18
sand gaper 26
sandpipers 43
Sargasso Sea 9
scallops 26, 29
schools (of fish) 30
scrimshaw 47, 61
scuba diving 21, 32
scurvy 48
sea anemones 17, 28, 29,
    42-43, 44
sea coconut 19
sea cucumbers 26, 27
sea grasses 26, 33
sea levels 40
sea lily 26
sea lions 32
sea mouse 29
sea otter 32, 58-59
sea pens 24, 26
sea slugs 29, 44
sea snakes 32
sea squirts 26, 43
sea urchins 26, 29, 31, 42, 43,
    44
seabirds (general) 37
seafloor sediments 16
seahorses 31
seals 15, 22, 30,
    bearded 23

elephant 32
fur 32
grey 26
harp 33
monk 59
Weddell 33
seawater 13
seaweeds 22, 26, 52
sextant 48, 61
sharks 23, 26, 30
shipwrecks 51
shrimps 27
soldierfish 44
Soucoupe Plongeante 21
spawning 44
Spider 20
spiny lobster 38, 39, 44
spits 40
sponges 27, 28, 43
spoonbills 43
spring tides 12, 61
starfish 26, 29, 42, 43, 44, 45
steamships 10
stromatolites 24, 61
squid 23, 29
submarines 20
submersibles 17, 20-21, 61
subduction zones 18
Suez Canal 10
surgeonfish 44
swim bladder 30, 60
swordfish 30

T

temperature (of oceans) 13
terns 36, 37, 38-39
Tethys ocean 18-19
thermal vents 17, 26, 61
thermocline 12, 26, 61
tidal power 53
tidal range 12-13, 61
tidal waves 19
tides 12-13
Titanic 21
toothed wrack 26
tourism 53
Trieste 21
trilobites 25
tripod fish 26-27
Truk Lagoon 51
tuna 27
turbidity currents 41, 61

U

upwellings 8-9, 26, 36, 51, 61

V

volcanic islands 15, 17, 19

W

water cycle 10
walrus 33
waterspouts 11, 61
waves 11, 41
    high ('freak') 10
    tidal 41
Weddell Sea 9
whales 22, 34-35
    belugas 33, 35, 57
    finback 34
    flensing 34
    Gray's 26
    grey 13, 34, 38
    minke 26
    Moby Dick 15
    orca (killer whale) 35
    pilot 34
    right 34
    sperm 6, 15, 21
whale-watching 58-59
whaling 34-35, 47
whelk shell 26
whirlpool 12, 15, 61
worms 24, 43
    bristle 42
    Christmas tree 28
    marine 28-29
    scale 26
    sea mouse 29

Z

zooplankton 27